LASSOED BY THE LAWMAN

TEXAS RANGER SERIES ~ BOOK 3

RENAE BRUMBAUGH GREEN

WILD HEART
BOOKS

Copyright © 2021 by Renae Brumbaugh Green

All rights reserved. No portion of this book may be reproduced or transmitted in any form or by any means—photocopied, shared electronically, scanned, stored in a retrieval system, or other—without the express permission of the publisher. Exceptions will be made for brief quotations used in critical reviews or articles promoting this work.

The characters and events in this fictional work are the product of the author's imagination. Any resemblance to actual people, living or dead, is coincidental.

Unless otherwise indicated, all Scripture quotations are taken from the Holy Bible, Kings James Version.

Cover design by: Carpe Librum Book Design

ISBN-13: 978-1-942265-33-7

To Vicki.
Sometimes family shows up in unexpected ways.
I'm so glad you showed up in my life.

"I thank God for you every time I think of you."
Philippians 1:3

CHAPTER 1

"Sing to the Lord a new song, for he has done marvelous things."
Psalm 98:1

May, 1882
South Texas

Cody Steves released Atlas's reins, adjusted his guitar, and strummed. He'd waited a month of Tuesdays for a moment like this—all alone on the range. It was the *range* part of *ranger* that drew him to the job.

That, and wanting to uphold the law.

He checked the position of the sun to verify the shortcut he hoped would cut an hour or more off his time. The bigger-than-life Texas sky, streaked with orange and gold and a hint of purple, soothed him, lulled him.

This...this was why he loved south Texas.

The crowded city of Houston behind him, the Mexican border before him...he could get used to this landscape. He strummed one of his favorite cowboy songs—one he'd learned as a child—and since there wasn't a soul for miles, he sang.

Loud. After all, Atlas seemed to enjoy his concerts. He never said otherwise, anyway.

This was the reason he volunteered for far-away jobs. The fellows—the other Rangers—ribbed him about being "The Singing Texas Ranger," but he didn't care. Music relaxed him. He'd spent a good part of the last couple of weeks singing hymns and cowboy songs, even making up a few of his own. Someone once asked why he didn't become one of those traveling minstrels, and the truth was, he didn't rightly know. He loved music. It was as necessary to his spirit as Texas air to his cowboy lungs.

But he loved being a Ranger, too. When he first started, at age twenty, he made more than his share of mistakes. There were times he didn't think he'd last the year. Now, after five years on the job, he wasn't sure he could leave it. It was in his blood.

Making music was something he could do anywhere, anytime. But if he quit being a Ranger, he'd miss it. He thrummed a new chord and belted out a high note, because he could.

Cody saw the rattlesnake too late. Atlas spooked and jerked sideways.

The next instant, Cody was sailing through the air. His body landed on a bed of cactus, and pain screamed through him. The succulent plant cushioned his fall and nearly killed him in the process.

He lay there a long minute, holding his breath because breathing made it hurt more. What was the best way to get up without pushing the painful thorns further into his flesh? How far had Atlas run? Hopefully not far. Where was his guitar? And where was that blasted snake?

So much pain. He tried for a shallow breath.

At least no one was around to witness his humiliation. But then he heard horse's hooves, and they were too far away to be

Atlas's. He tried to stand, but pain seared him, stilling his efforts. That cactus had really got him good. He groped around for his gun.

A shadow moved over his face. He squinted into the sunlight, but all he could see was a silhouette.

A very feminine silhouette. Sitting atop a horse.

"Need a hand?" a silky voice spoke.

He wished she'd move around so he could see her face. "Looks that way."

She laughed then, a strong, rich laugh that reminded him of country church bells on a clear Easter morning.

He would have smiled, but pain refused him that pleasure. "I'm glad someone's entertained by my agony."

There it was again, that musical laugh. Muse-like, anyway. "I'm sorry. I'm not laughing at your pain. More at the performance that led up to it." She climbed from her horse then, and he could finally see her features. And despite his current discomfort, his heart became a newly-caught catfish, flipping and flopping all over his chest.

Standing over him was the most beautiful creature he'd ever seen.

~

*S*o, this was the Ranger her father had been waiting for. Julianna Duke knew without asking, by the star badge pinned to his vest. She tried not to stare at the long, cowboy legs or the way the fabric in his shirt pulled at his broad shoulders. Even lying in a cactus, the man was gorgeous.

Why was he way out here? Why hadn't he gone around, taken the entrance?

She held out a hand. "Might as well just get it over with. It'll hurt no matter what."

The man took her clasp and allowed her to help him to his

feet. To his credit, he didn't groan too awful loudly. "Did you see where my horse went?"

"That way, into those trees. But you won't be able to ride until those stickers come out."

The man turned around and pulled a few cactus thorns out of his pants, one at a time, wincing with each one.

"You can't get them all yourself. Trust me. I've tried."

"You've landed in cactus before?"

"Unfortunately, yes." She didn't offer any more explanation of her childhood mishap. "You're a Ranger."

"Uh... yeah. That'd be me. Lieutenant Cody Steves. I'm looking for Mr. Oscar Duke." He offered his hand, and she took it. "And you are...?"

Juliana stilled the shock that threatened her face, replacing it with a slow smile. He had no idea who she was!

He'd find out soon enough, but it wasn't often she got to be just plain old Juliana, and not Oscar Duke's daughter. It was a luxury she wasn't willing to part with, quite yet. "Juliana. I'll take you where you need to go." She backed up a step, toward Cielito, who chomped on a clump of bluestem grass.

"Much obliged. But I need to—" He froze, then reached for the pistol in his holster. "Don't move," he whispered, but his eyes stayed glued to some point behind her. That's when she heard it—the unmistakable *ts-ts-ts* of a rattlesnake's warning, right at the same time Cielito whinnied and shifted away.

In an instant, Cody fired, but she still didn't move. She had no idea how near the snake was, but dead rattlesnakes still carried venom. Could still bite. Could still be deadly. It took a few minutes for their brains to tell the rest of their bodies they were done.

After a moment, Cody crept forward, and she turned to see one beautiful, lethal diamond-back rattler, probably more than four feet long. Its back was checkered with astonishing reds and browns, and she could picture a dress print with a similar pattern. The creature wriggled and writhed not three feet from her skirt hem. After a heart-stopping eternity, it quit moving, and she let out a breath.

Cody made a move to kick the snake away, but she held up her arm. "No! Wait."

He looked at her like she was loco. She flipped open her saddlebag, grabbed her tablet and pencils, and began to sketch and shade. The image took shape quickly, and soon, she replaced the tablet. "All right. I'm done."

When she looked at him again, he hadn't moved. Just stood there, with an expression that made her wonder if he wanted to put her in an asylum.

Heat warmed her neck, but she shrugged. "You sing. I draw."

His expression changed then. He nodded, kicked the snake away, and picked his guitar off the ground. "Well, Miss Juliana-the-artist, I need to find Atlas, and we need to get out of here. Snakes have dens, you know. Where there's one rattlesnake, there may be another."

He placed his index fingers in his mouth and let out a shrill whistle. In just a moment, the big draft horse trotted from behind some brush on the side of a hill.

❧

Cody leaned forward in his saddle to keep from putting pressure on his backside and followed Juliana through a little trail in the valley, just wide enough for a single horse and rider. What was a girl like her doing way out in the middle of nowhere? Well, somewhere. The Duke Ranch, specifically.

She was probably a ranch hand's daughter. Still, she shouldn't be out alone. Especially when Duke was looking for bandits. "So you heard my concert, did you?" he called.

She laughed again. A man could get used to a laugh like that. "Yes...I heard. You have a nice singing voice, Señor Steves."

"Thank you. I wasn't aware I had an audience."

"Would it have made a difference?"

Cody chuckled. "Probably not."

"Do you always sing cowboy songs, or do you perform other types of music, as well?" She glanced over her shoulder.

"Oh, I sing all kinds of music. Even write some of my own."

"Really? Sing me something you wrote."

Hmm... He was best at making up impromptu songs, but usually didn't write them down, so he'd forgotten most of them. Without his guitar—he couldn't hold it at the angle he sat—he felt a little lost, but that was all right.

In his deepest, loudest voice, he sang:

There once was a Ranger
Who fought against danger
With a guitar and a strong set o' lungs.
He needed some practice,
But he fell on a cactus,
And now, instead of singin', he hums.

Juliana hooted. "Stop! You're making me cry."

"It's that bad?"

She laughed harder, an adorable sound. "Stop it!"

Atlas went over a bump, and Cody flinched. He'd heard laughter was good medicine, but Juliana's was about the best pain reliever he'd ever had. The way she leaned her head back and laughed from deep in her gut, yet the sound was still entirely feminine. It made him want to try anything to keep the sound coming.

His mind spun with words to a song about this woman on a horse. But he dare not sing it for her—it would embarrass them both. That fall must have rattled his brain more than he realized.

Right now, he had a job to do. There was an unwritten code

among the Rangers—never mix work with pleasure. Specifically, female pleasure. Women could distract a man, cloud his thoughts. He forced his mind away from the curvy figure ahead of him and onto the reason for his journey.

The Duke Ranch. Bandits.

Before long, they rounded a bend in the road and a magnificent two-story house appeared, a cool refuge in the parched desert. A porch wrapped around every side, and white columns held up a wrap-around balcony on the second floor.

An immaculate yard was lush with grass and shrubbery, and walkways meandered here and there through miniature gardens of bright native flowers. He recognized bougainvillea and Mexican birds of paradise, along with lantana, salvia, Mexican heather, and several varieties he couldn't identify.

Off to one side, lily pads bloomed bright pink in a small pond, and from his position in Atlas's saddle, he could see goldfish. Benches nestled here and there in shady spots, giving the place a fancy resort feel.

But this was no resort. This was someone's home. *My, oh my.* What some land and a whole lot of money could create.

Two men sat on the porch, the older one holding a glass of what looked like lemonade. They both stood, and the younger fellow bounded down the stairs toward Juliana.

"Hello, Miguel." Juliana greeted the younger man, then looked to the older one. "Papa, I want you both to meet Lieutenant Cody Steves, of the Texas Rangers. Lt. Steves, this is Miguel Fuentes, our ranch foreman. And this is Oscar Duke. My father."

Cody climbed from Atlas and extended his hand, trying his hardest not to cringe at the pain in his posterior. But even more than the thorns, he had to keep his face from showing the shock that shimmied up his spine and down again.

Juliana was a Duke.

uliana saw the moment her identity registered with Cody. He'd been all smiles and twinkly eyes and dimples, and ah! How she'd love to draw those golden eyes, those deep dimples.

But the moment she introduced Papa, he changed. His posture stiffened, and there was that ever-so-brief hint of surprise as he looked from her father to her, then back again. After that, he transformed from happy-go-lucky cowboy to down-to-business lawman.

Of course, it could be that now he was on duty, where before he'd just been himself. Relaxed. Fun-loving. But Juliana had lived a lifetime of being Oscar Duke's heiress, and that was plenty long enough to know people treated her differently simply because of her last name. They were *nicer* to her, because she was a Duke. And yet, they *weren't* as nice to her, because she was a Duke.

Careful distance. Politeness. From everyone. It was exhausting.

For a few minutes, she'd just been Juliana. She'd laughed out loud and talked and flirted with an incredibly handsome man, and... And it had been nice while it lasted.

At least Miguel didn't treat her differently. But Miguel was practically family. They'd grown up together. Climbed trees and gone fishing and gotten in trouble for sneaking a bucket of mud to the upstairs playroom so they could make mudpies. Her parents wanted her to marry Miguel. He'd already asked for her hand...several times. But for some reason, she just couldn't get too excited at the thought of marrying her brother.

Cody Steves, on the other hand... He was someone she could wrap her heart around. Except now, he wasn't interested.

"I expected you to come from the opposite direction," Papa said as he led Cody up the stairs toward the front door. "Miguel will see to your horse. I'm sure you're exhausted. Come inside, and I'll see you get a cool drink and a hot meal."

"Papa, he's injured. He fell in the cactus."

Cody looked at her with gaze narrowed as if to say, *Silencio.* But she knew all too well, if those thorns weren't removed, they could get infected.

Papa looked at her, then at Cody. "You don't say? How did that happen?"

Red crept up Cody's neck. "Uh. My horse spoo—"

"There was a rattlesnake, Papa. Right behind me. The lieutenant shot it. He probably saved my life." There. Maybe that would soothe his wounded ego.

"Really? You saved my little girl's life?" Papa clapped Cody on the back. "Let's get you inside, Ranger. Miguel, run up to the bunkhouse and tell José to come. And bring his tweezers."

Cody followed Papa into the house, and Juliana trailed behind. But the wounded Ranger refused to look at her. Was it her identity, or his embarrassment about the cactus that caused his personality to turn from a warm south wind to a cool norther?

She didn't know the answer, but one thing she was sure of. An hour ago, Cody Steves had been interested in her. Now, he wasn't.

CHAPTER 2

"Pride goes before destruction, and a haughty spirit before a fall."
Proverbs 16:18

Forty-five humiliating minutes later, Cody was cactus—and pride—free. José, as it turned out, was the ranch cook, medicine man, and José-of-all-trades. At least the man had a sense of humor. While he tweezed, he fired jokes and funny stories. Cody even learned about Juliana's cactus experience when she was seven years old.

He also learned José was Miguel's father, and had been the ranch foreman until last year, when he injured his back and could no longer ride a horse for long periods.

"That's when Miguel took over?"

"*Sí.* He is young—only twenty-four—but he's done the job by my side since he was seventeen. I'm hoping, as are Mr. and Mrs. Duke, that Miguel will be more than foreman one day."

"What do you mean?"

José laughed. "Ahhh, Miguel and Juliana. They were made for one another. She is still young, but someday... Well, I've said

10

too much. I'm done now. Get dressed. You'll be sore for a few days, but you'll live."

Cody felt a sting in his heart that rivaled the one in his backside. At least he knew where things stood with Juliana. Not that it mattered. She was a distraction he didn't need. Besides, she was an heiress. He could never offer her anything close to this kind of life.

Miguel and Mr. Duke waited on the porch. "All better now?" The older man's voice held a spark of humor.

"Good as new, sir. Why don't you fill me in on these cattle rustlers? I need to know how many times your property has been invaded, where they're getting in, and how many head of cattle have been stolen."

The man's expression sobered. "I'd say six hundred or more. They're getting in different ways. Our property borders the Gulf of Mexico, but we've got it fenced several hundred feet in from the water's edge. Still, some of our men feel the thieves could be coming from Mexico or the United States, using a cattle barge."

"Can a barge carry that many cattle?" Cody had heard of such things, but it was hard to imagine.

"If it's big enough, it can hold quite a few. The boats are brought over from Europe, where they're used in trade and can carry several tons of cargo. Depending on the wind, they can go pretty fast, too."

Cody shook his head. It was one thing to secure land. Another to secure the Gulf of Mexico. "I'd like to see the property and where you think they're getting in."

Duke nodded. "Miguel plans to take you on a tour first thing in the morning. But for now, let's get you settled and rested."

Miguel stood. "I'll show you the bunkhouse, where I've already placed your things."

"There's been a change in plans," Duke said. "Lt. Steves saved

Juliana's life. He's staying in the house with us. It's the least I can do."

Cody cleared his throat. "Thank you, sir. But you don't need to do that. The bunkhouse is fine. It's probably nicer than what I have at home."

Duke put up his hand. "It's settled. Miguel, bring his things. Ranger, follow me." He pushed up from the white rocking chair, took his lemonade, and opened the front door. "Maria! Our guest is ready for his room."

~

Juliana ran the dusting cloth over the mahogany wood in one of their many guest rooms. More of a suite, really, this room was decorated with deer and elk antlers, and the head and fur of a black bear hung on one wall. Her mother figured Lt. Steves would like it here.

If Juliana had known her little confession about Cody saving her life would get him the royal treatment, she'd have...done it again. Maybe now, she'd have more contact with the handsome Ranger.

She moved from the dresser to the chest-of-drawers. People had the wrong idea about what it meant to be *her*. Most people assumed servants waited on her. Truth was, Mama didn't believe in many servants. While they did employ enough men to run the ranch and offered jobs to those men's family members when possible, Mama liked to run her own household.

Duke Ranch had been handed down to Papa from his father and grandfather, and the Duke men were no strangers to hard work, either. Papa loved to tell the story of how he met Mama on a cattle drive. One of the cows got lost, and he went in search of her. He never found the cow, but he did find Mama, washing clothes in the Rio Grande. She spoke about five or six English words then, and Papa spoke about that much Spanish.

Apparently, that was enough for them to fall in love and get married.

They still acted more like youngsters around each other than old married people. Juliana sighed. She wanted that kind of love. Surely her parents wanted that for her, as well. She knew they did. They just thought she could have it with Miguel.

And maybe she could have, if she'd never experienced the sweet-hot explosion in her spirit that was set off today. She closed her eyes and recalled her mind's picture of Cody, just after she'd helped him to his feet.

This man, six-foot-four if he was an inch, blond hair flopped over one eye and curled up at the neck, grin quirked up more on one side, revealing a single, crooked canine tooth. This man whose expression seemed to hide a private joke, whose baby-smooth cheeks belied his crinkle-framed, honey-colored eyes, star-shaped badge pinned to his chest, gun holstered at his hip, whose shoulders pulled the plaid lines in his shirt at odd angles, whose wing span looked to cover two counties, who looked more mischief-maker than law defender. *This* was the man Juliana wanted to know better.

"Juliana. Your papa just called from below. Is the room ready?"

"Sí, Mama. I think Lt. Steves will be very comfortable here."

"*Bueno*. I'm going to meet him now. Come with me or go somewhere else. It's not proper for you to be in the man's bedroom when he arrives."

"I'll be right down. I have to stop by my room for a moment."

"*¡Ándalé!*" Mama called over her shoulder.

Juliana's hummingbird heart pounded in rhythm with her feet as she flew through the door at the far end of the hall that led to the family quarters and shut it behind her.

In her room, she checked her reflection. Oh, my, she was a mess. No wonder Cody hadn't given her a second look once they'd arrived. Should she change dresses? Was there time, with all she still had to do? And if she did change her dress, would it look like she was trying too hard, like she wanted to impress him?

Which she wasn't. Trying to impress him. Absolutely not. If he didn't like her when she was a mess, he wasn't worth impressing.

In a flash, she tugged her current dress over her head and flung the garment on the bed. Then she pulled out her favorite creation—a flowing cotton dress of bright blues and yellows, with a scarf sash. She'd finished it just last week. The neckline was wide and high. Not off the shoulders at all, like some of the Mexican fashions, but wide enough to give that impression without being immodest.

She held her breath—as if that would speed up the process—while she ran a brush through her tangled curls and tied them back with a matching blue ribbon. No, she didn't like that. She took it down, then scooped the ribbon from beneath her hairline at the neck to the top of her head, tying a bow and leaving her hair long and loose.

Perfect.

She pinched her cheeks and bit her lips to make them rosy, then fled out the door and down the front stairs, pausing halfway to catch her breath.

❧

The guest room the Duke family offered was larger than Cody's entire house. He smiled his appreciation to Mrs. Duke and Juliana, who trailed her mother, then looked back at the mounted grizzly on the wall. The creature was impressive. Plus, it gave him something to look at other than the stunning heiress in the blue dress.

The quicker he captured the rustlers and got them behind bars, the quicker he could be done with this torture of having to be near the most attractive woman he'd ever met, knowing she could never be his. Even if he wasn't on duty, it could never work. She was far above his station.

Not that Miguel was in her station. But clearly, that had all been arranged. Funny though. Why was Miss Duke here with him instead of batting those thick eyelashes at her intended?

José had commented about her age, though he'd not stated the number exactly. She didn't look that young to him—maybe nineteen or twenty—but maybe she was younger than she looked. *That must be it. She's probably sixteen. And they're waiting for her to come of age before they marry her off.* Good night! He nearly lost his mind over a child. Heat surged up his neck as he felt every kind of foolish.

Better keep his distance. He needed to get back out on the open range. He'd rather face lowlifes and scallywags and slithery reptiles than this breathtaking, under-age heiress who probably made a game of wooing every man she met. As big as this house was, her presence stifled him.

"Do you have everything you need, Lt. Steves?" Mrs. Duke's accent was enthralling. Juliana had a trace of the same accent, though not as strong.

"Yes, ma'am. It's all very nice. I'll be more than comfortable here."

"*Muy bueno.*" The woman looked around the room. "Juliana, Lt. Steves needs some *agua*. Go get him a pitcher of water and a glass."

"That's not necessary, ma'am. I'll be fine."

"*Tonterias.* Nonsense. We will have a meal for you in half an hour, but a working man should never go thirsty. We'll leave you to get settled, and Juliana will be back with some water, *pronto.*"

If he'd learned one thing from his mother, it was to never argue with a matriarch. "Yes, ma'am. Thank you."

"De nada." The woman whisked from the room, followed by the flash of blue that was her daughter.

When the door shut, Cody took his eyes off the bear and flopped on the bed. Even with the soft mattress, he flinched at the soreness in his backside. But a cactus wound was the least of his problems.

A few minutes later, when the knock on the door sounded, he opened it just enough to take the glass and pitcher. He thanked Juliana without looking at her and closed the door.

~

If Juliana had had any question about whether Lt. Cody Steves found her attractive, she didn't anymore. Why, the man barely looked at her. And to think, she'd been saving this dress for someone special. What a waste.

It was probably best. She certainly didn't have time to moon over some good-looking Ranger. She had sketches to draw and dresses to sew in between her household chores and ranch duties. She had no desire to pine for someone who wasn't even interested in her.

Mama wanted her in the kitchen to help set the table. Should she change her dress to keep from getting anything on it? Why bother? If the gown was soiled, it was soiled. The only people to ever see it, or any of her other creations, were the folks on this ranch. Unless, of course, she decided to wear it out to herd.

Now that was a thought. She could wear a new dress every time she went with Miguel to help with roundup. Hundreds, no thousands of pairs of eyes would see her dresses then. The fact that those eyes belonged to cattle was moot. If she was going to be a *vaquera,* she'd be the best dressed vaquera on the Duke Ranch.

Which didn't say much, considering she was the only cowgirl she knew.

CHAPTER 3

"So whether you eat or drink, or whatever you do, do it all for the glory of God."
1 Corinthians 10:31

*D*inner wasn't as formal as Cody expected. He'd washed and changed into clean denims and a fresh button-up shirt. But when he entered the cavernous dining room, he found Mr. Duke wearing the same clothes he'd worn earlier. Miguel and José were present, as well. Ramona Fuentes, Miguel's mother, bustled alongside Mrs. Duke and Juliana. The women placed steaming bowls of rice and beans and freshly baked tortillas on the table. It felt more like a family supper than a fancy dinner.

"There you are!" Mrs. Duke welcomed him. "Have a seat there across from José. Sí, right there. Juliana, pour him some tea."

Juliana came near, and the smell of lavender preceded her. Man, he'd rather be in the bunkhouse with a bunch of smelly ranch hands right about now.

Mr. Duke settled in his chair. "So, Lt. Steves. How long have you been a part of the Texas Ranger force?"

Grateful for the diversion, Cody shifted in his seat to face the man fully, so his back was to Juliana. "Five years."

"Do you have experience with cattle rustlers?"

Cody nodded. "It's a pretty common problem, no matter where you go in Texas. I must say, however, this is the largest ranch I've worked on. Have you been in contact with your local law enforcement at all?" He assumed they had, but he wanted to keep the conversation moving.

The man nodded. "Our local sheriff, John Gardner, has been on the case since the first incident. He's stationed in Brownsville, a few miles from our southern border."

"You said they're getting in at a different place each time?"

"*Qué es esto?*" Mrs. Duke scolded as she placed a meat-filled platter on the table. "Oscar, our guest has traveled many days. He's—how you say?—exhausted. Let us talk of something else."

"It's quite all right, ma'am. I'm anxious to find out what I can," Cody assured her.

"Best not to argue with any woman, Ranger, but especially not one who speaks Spanish." Duke winked at his wife. "She can rapidfire those words so fast your head'll feel like a tornado hit it. You'll have no idea what she said, but trust me...you'll know she won."

"*Me alegro tanto de qué intiende!*" Mrs. Duke called from the kitchen. "I'm so glad you understand."

Cody laughed at Mr. and Mrs. Duke's easy banter. This scene wasn't what he'd expected of the Duke dynasty. That flash of blue passed by on the other side of the table, so he focused instead on the platter of meat. "Everything looks and smells delicious."

Mrs. Duke entered from the kitchen, followed by Mrs. Fuentes. "*Muchas gracias*, Lt. Steves. I hope it tastes to your liking. Juliana, you sit by the Ranger, across from Miguel."

"Yes, Mama."

Wonderful. This arrangement wouldn't help his sanity any. Or his control.

As they bowed their heads for prayer, Cody offered a silent request that he'd find those rustlers soon. If not, this could become his most challenging assignment yet.

~

*H*ad Juliana done something to offend the Ranger? Surely he wasn't upset because she didn't tell him right away who she was. Was he?

She replayed every second in her mind, from the moment she offered to help him up from the cactus until she accompanied Mama to show him his room. Once he arrived at the house, he turned from hot pepper to cold fish.

Oh, he was polite. Had impeccable manners. At dinner, when they passed around the platters, he held each dish for her while she dipped her serving, then passed it across to Miguel. But gone was the funny, quirky singing cowboy she thought she'd met. In his place was an aloof lawman who spoke only when spoken to.

Well, Juliana could be cool and polite just like he could.

How could a man she'd only met a few hours before make her feel so discombobulated? At least tomorrow, he'd be out of the house working. It was silly, anyway, to get all excited about a near-perfect stranger.

If only he weren't so near perfect...

"Juliana. Did you hear me?"

Oh, dear. "Sorry, Mama. I was lost in my head. *Repita, por favor?*"

For some reason, everyone laughed. "Sí, I will repeat. You seem distracted. What is filling your mind today?"

Juliana sat taller and tried to pretend Cody Steves wasn't

next to her. This was her home. Her table. No need to impress someone who clearly didn't want to be impressed.

"I've been working on some new drawings."

"*Ay, mi.* What are we going to do with you? More dresses, I suppose."

"Yes, more dresses. But I've been thinking...what if I made some clothes for each of the ranch wives and daughters? We could have a party, and they'd all have something new to wear."

"That's a lovely thought, *mi hija dulce.* But that would take a very long time."

"Perhaps I could hire an assistant?"

Everyone laughed again. To those sitting at the table, her designs were a cute hobby. Something to pass the time.

"How many dresses would that be?" Cody asked.

"Between three and four dozen."

"And you want to design an original dress for each woman or girl?"

At last. He sounded genuinely interested. But was he just being polite? "Yes. I—"

"That girl of mine has her head in the clouds," Papa said. "Nearly twenty years old, and she's so heavenly minded, she's no earthly good." He laughed and sent her a wink.

She knew Papa was only teasing. Still, it hurt to have him cut her off like that.

Cody didn't laugh with the rest of them. "Your daughter must be very talented."

"She is," Miguel answered, a hint of challenge in his voice. "Juliana has many talents. She plays the piano and sings beautifully, in addition to designing dresses."

The table quieted, as if everyone waited for Cody's response. After a moment, he said, "Mr. Duke, it appears all the women in your family have talent. This is the most delicious meal I've had in a long time." He pushed his empty plate away from him as if to emphasize his satisfaction.

"I agree. And Miguel brought up a good point. Juliana, why don't you play something for us? You've been so wrapped up in your drawings lately, you've neglected your music."

"Oh, no, Papa. I really don't—"

"Nonsense. You should play for our guest. Sing something."

A grin sneaked across her face. "Perhaps our guest can perform for us. He was singing and strumming his guitar when I found him."

~

*D*id she really just volunteer him to sing? All eyes turned from Juliana to Cody, and he felt hunted. Exposed.

"Is this true, Lt. Steves? You are a musician?" Delight bloomed on Mrs. Duke's face.

Cody cleared his throat. "I...wouldn't call myself a true musician. I play and sing a little."

"Very well, then. We shall have a concert. Lt. Steves, go and get your guitar, and Juliana will accompany you on the piano. You both will sing." Mrs. Duke was a small woman, but she certainly had a commanding presence. Kind of like her daughter.

"Yes, ma'am." He scooted his chair away from the table. He'd just been issued a direct order.

Ten minutes later, Cody stood near the piano with his guitar, looking over Juliana's shoulder at the hymnal from which she played. Their voices blended in harmony as she sang melody with her alto voice and he added the tenor.

What a friend we have in Jesus,
All our sins and griefs to bear!
What a privilege to carry
Everything to God in prayer!

Oh, what peace we often forfeit,
Oh, what needless pain we bear,
All because we do not carry
Everything to God in prayer!

They sang the remaining three verses. When the last note carried through the warm, South Texas wind, a hush captured their audience. There was something sweet and pure and holy in that moment, like they'd been to church.

Miguel broke the silence with his whispered, "That was beautiful, Juliana." To his credit, he stood and reached for Cody's hand. "Well done, Ranger."

But he squeezed Cody's hand a little too tightly, and the tension around his jawline said what the man's words didn't. *Back off. She's mine.*

CHAPTER 4

"When you lie down, you will not be afraid. When you rest, your sleep
will be peaceful."
Proverbs 3:24

Cody lay in bed, as wide awake as a coyote on a coon hunt. Juliana was almost twenty? Closer to his original estimation. Why wasn't she already married? Miguel was clearly ready to call Juliana his own.

Maybe she didn't love him? And if so, maybe...

No. Juliana could never love a man like Cody, with barely a place to lay his head. He couldn't give her anything close to what her father could provide. Besides, what would he do with a woman? Take her with him on assignment? Leave her in constant fear of becoming a widow?

Their duet tonight played through his memory like a lullaby, only instead of lulling him to sleep, it kept him from it. There was an undeniable connection there.

Of course, there would be. She was a creative soul, like Cody. He didn't meet too many of those in his line of work. But just because they'd had a moment—okay, a couple of moments

23

—didn't justify losing his heart and an entire night's sleep, over what? A pretty face?

When the sun's first pink rays streaked through the clouds, Cody was already up and dressed. Had Atlas fed, watered and saddled. He waited on the porch for Miguel, who was supposed to give him the grand tour.

"Good. I see you're ready," Miguel called from the barn's shadows. "I like to get an early start."

Cody fought back a yawn, stretched from the white painted rocker, and clomped down the front steps. "Me too."

Within the hour, rivalry gave way to camaraderie of shared concern. The place was twice the size of Houston. How could one man, or even a few, secure such a vast spread? With one side bordering the Gulf of Mexico?

"Sheriff Gardner's been on the case over a month now. He's assigned two deputies, as well, but they have other responsibilities. We've all done our best, but it's not like the other cattle will wait for us to solve this crime. They have constant needs. That's why Señor Duke sent for you. We hope, since this is your only obligation, you'll be able to capture whoever is responsible."

Cody squinted into the sun. "I'll do my best. I hope I'm up to the task."

"I hope so too. *Dios estara con usted.*"

"Pardon?"

Miguel reined his horse in at the top of a ridge. "It's just a saying we have. It means, *God will be with you.*"

Cody nodded and looked at the vast range. "He'll have to be."

❧

"Shhhhh. It's all right, *pobrecita.* Poor baby. I know it hurts." Juliana kept her voice a low monotone, one arm completely submerged in the animal. The heifer had tried to calve for several hours now, and something was wrong.

José stood behind her. "Do you feel the head?"

"No. I think it's breeched." She removed her arm and accepted the towel José handed her, then washed in the nearby bucket.

Mama wiped sweat off her worry-lined brow with a faded red bandana. "Go get Miguel. He'll know what to do."

"Where's Papa?"

"He's at the north fence today. Miguel was to ride the ridge with Lt. Steves—he's closer." Mama knelt next to the ailing cow.

Juliana flew to the stable and climbed onto Cielito, bareback. "Hyah!"

Cielito sensed her urgency and charged ahead, full speed. A short time later, she spotted two riders on the ridge. She drew back her tongue and pushed her bottom jaw forward to force out the piercing tooth whistle she'd perfected at age twelve. Mama had scolded her then. But…for such a time as this.

Sure enough, both riders headed toward her, Miguel in the lead. Even before either had reined in, she called, "Breech birth!" Miguel spurred his horse again and headed homeward, leaving Juliana with Cody. And her looking a mess.

"Do you need to return, as well?" he asked, his eyes flitting across her sticky, bloody blouse.

"No. I'd only be in the way at this point."

"Breech birth, eh? You think Miguel can save the calf?"

"He's done it before. Cow and calf lived. He'll have to cut her open."

Cody nodded. Turned his head to look back at the ridge.

"Did you finish your tour?"

"No. That's all right. I've got a starting point now."

She clicked to Cielito. "Come. I'll show you the rest." Cielito trotted, and for a moment, she wondered if Cody would follow. After a time, he clucked to Atlas and trailed her.

For nearly ten minutes, neither spoke. Yet it didn't feel awkward at all. She paused to let the horses drink from a diamond-shimmered stream and breathed in the scent of pine mixed with oak. A mosquito sang an off-key tune near her face, and she swatted at the insect.

"That was some whistle back there," Cody finally broke the silence.

"Sí. It's one of my better skills."

"You seem to be a lady of many talents."

"Just a few."

"Oh, I don't know about that. There aren't too many ladies who can draw, sew, sing, play the piano, cook, whistle, *and* help birth a calf." His eyes sparked, and that grin quirked up to the left.

This was the man she'd met yesterday. "I enjoyed singing with you last night. I haven't played in a while. I tend to get focused on one task, and I forget about everything else for a while."

"Right now, it's your drawing?"

"Sort of. I've always sketched and designed dresses, for as long as I can remember. That never really goes away. But right now, I'm also drawing nature. Sometimes I incorporate the patterns into my dresses. But music...it's a love of mine, too."

"You play well. You pour your soul into the keys."

"Thank you. I enjoy playing what's on the page, but I've never written my own music, like you do."

"Have you tried?"

"No. I don't know why. I never really thought about it."

"As creative as you are, you should give it a go."

They rode for another stretch without talking. It felt nice, just enjoying the day. After a time, Cody guided Atlas beside her. "Back to that whistle. It hurt my ears." He gave a mock grimace. "Were you born with that gift, or did you have to prac-tice it?"

"I practiced for a month before I could make any sound

come out. That was years ago. Are you going to write a song about the whistling vaquera now?"

He laughed. "Oh, I could. But I have a feeling there's a lot more to learn about this whistling cowgirl. I'll have to watch a while longer, to make sure I don't miss anything."

"Chicken."

"Really? You think I'm afraid to write a song about you?"

"I don't know. Maybe you're afraid you can't come up with a rhyme for *whistle*."

Cody cleared his throat, sat up taller in his saddle, and bellowed,

> *"There once was a cowgirl who whistled,*
> *She rescued me from a sharp thistle,*
> *She rode like the sky, and she . . .*

Juliana laughed. "See?"

A twinkle touched his gaze as he continued.

> *"She rode like the sky, delivered calves and baked pie,*
> *And the cowboys all wanted a kissel!"*

She couldn't hold back the smile that spread across her face like melted butter on hot bread.

And there, for a flash, their eyes met. Held.

Like a lightning bug, it was gone. A shadow passed his rugged features, and he pulled his eyes away. "I believe this is as far as we got before, Miss Duke. Show me where the property goes from here."

~

*J*uliana proved an apt guide. She not only showed him the boundaries and some places the rustlers might have breeched, but also points of interest along the way.

"A herd of wild mustangs lives beyond that ridge. We've tried to catch some, but they won't be caught. Now we leave them alone."

"Wild mustangs, eh? That would be a sight to see."

A glint sparked her eye. "Follow me." She clicked to Cielito and was off. *Wind and sky*, he thought as he remembered her horse's name.

"Come on, Atlas!" he urged, but they struggled to catch the smaller horse and rider. He gave the horse his head, tightened his grip on the reins, and for just a moment, loosened his grip on his swirling emotions. Juliana was a moving masterpiece. Her hair, her patterned skirt, her porcelain-smooth skin all fit with the landscape of mature oaks, quail, and whitetail deer, both wild and beautiful.

They topped another ridge, and a small valley came into view. There, a stunning herd of mustangs ran away from them, manes and tails whipping in the wind.

"Wow," Cody breathed, more to himself than to her.

"I love to watch them. I only wish they'd let me get closer. But any time a human approaches, they disappear into caves and around crags and crevices. We call these the Mustang Caves."

Caves, crags, and crevices. All ideal hiding places for rustlers. As if in answer to his thought, a single rider appeared from behind a tall rock. Alarm rose in Cody. He needed to get Juliana away from here.

But she waved her arms. "It's Sheriff Gardner!" she exclaimed and headed into the valley.

Cody trailed behind. No one had mentioned the sheriff

would be out today. Then again, since he'd already been asked to assist with the case, maybe he didn't need special permission to be on the property.

"Sheriff Gardner," Juliana spoke to the man when she neared.

"Juliana. What are you doing way out here? And who is this?" The man squinted in Cody's direction.

"This is Lt. Cody Steves of the Texas Rangers. Papa requested his assistance. He knows how busy you are. Lt. Steves, this is Sheriff John Gardner."

A shadow passed over the man's face. Cody was used to that. Local law enforcement often resented the Rangers' presence. They viewed it as an insult to their abilities to handle cases. Cody held out his hand. "Sheriff Gardner, I'm pleased to meet you. I'm a bit overwhelmed at the size of this place. I can use all the help I can get. I'll be glad to assist you in any way, as well." Meeting other law enforcement was always a bit awkward, but he tried to be as gracious as possible. Sometimes, the biggest skeptics turned into fierce allies.

Gardner looked at Cody's hand a moment before shaking it, and a tentative half-smile broke away from the frown. "Likewise."

"We were about to head back to the house for our mid-day meal. Would you care to join us, Sheriff?" Juliana's voice flowed, a desert stream on a sun-scorched day.

"No, thank you. I'd love to taste more of your Mama's cooking, but I need to get back to town. I had a little time, so I thought I'd check out this part of the property again, see if I missed anything."

"As always, thank you for your assistance, Sheriff," Juliana said. "Tell Emily hello for me. I wish she'd come visit more often."

"I'll do that. I'm sure she'd love to see you."

Juliana nodded to Cody. "We'd best be going. We'll be late as it is." Like a flash, she guided Cielito out of the valley, up the steep incline to the ridge.

Cody nodded to the sheriff and followed Juliana. Despite the day's heat, the reception here was a bit cool. Besides, he was hungry.

~

*J*uliana relished the breeze on her face and tried to make sense of her turbulent thoughts. As she rode, she surveyed the property that would one day be hers—was already hers. It really was beautiful. She'd done nothing to deserve this privileged life she led, other than be born. It wasn't such a bad life. Why did she want to escape it?

Miguel's face scooted across her mind. Dear Miguel. He was a good man. He'd make a good husband. Why couldn't she want *him?* Cody's face crowded her thoughts, pushing Miguel's away. She could easily see what drew her to Cody...he was handsome, and his spirit seemed to fit hers like a matched puzzle piece. But there were other pieces to this puzzle, and Cody couldn't fill in all those holes like Miguel could. If she didn't marry Miguel, who would take over the ranch?

She didn't stop at the stable, but rode right into the barn to check on the birth. Cody didn't follow her.

There was Miguel, feeding a new calf with a bottle. It was beautiful, but bittersweet. "You couldn't save the heifer?"

He shook his head. "She was too far gone. This one's foot was all the way through her uterus. She'd lost too much blood."

Juliana climbed from Cielito, looped his reins around a post, and approached the man and calf. "May I?"

Miguel handed her the bottle. The calf looked at her with frightened eyes that seemed too large for his face and sucked fiercely.

"I hate she died. But feeding a calf is one of my favorite chores."

Miguel leaned forward, his chin just above her ear. "You'll make a good mama someday."

She knew what he implied. Knew what he longed for. Could she give it to him?

Maybe becoming a wife and mother would open the path to that new adventure she longed for. Even if she couldn't own a dress shop, she could sew curtains for her home and clothes for her children and . . .

Miguel moved away and said nothing more. She knew he waited for her signal, her nod of approval to proceed with the marriage that everyone expected but nobody discussed. At least not in front of her.

Perhaps it was time.

~

Unlike dinner last night, lunch was served in a massive dining hall, with several dozen ranch hands in attendance. Cody was introduced to all of them, but had a hard time keeping their names straight. Gabe, Isaac, Jim. Fred and Cade. A dozen more he couldn't recall. They circled the perimeter of the room when Mr. Duke called them to order. None had to be told to bow their heads before their boss led in prayer.

"Father, thank You for every person here, and for the food we're about to eat. Be with us and keep us safe. Protect our borders and help us stop those rustlers from getting any more cattle. Amen."

Cody liked the way the man prayed. Short and to the point.

His eyes wandered to Juliana. She'd changed into a fresh dress, and her presence seeped into his senses like hot soup on a cold day.

How she'd gotten such a stronghold on his thoughts, he

didn't know. Marriage and rangering didn't go well together. He'd watched other Rangers get married. He'd also watched their wives worry themselves sick every time their husbands took a new assignment. He'd even seen a few widows and orphans left behind.

He loved being a Ranger. If that meant giving up marriage and family, so be it. He had Atlas. And he had his guitar.

But if he had a woman like Juliana waiting at home for him every night... Mercy. He really did need to rein in his thoughts. She was an heiress...and already spoken for. This morning's playful song-session was absolutely out of line. From now on, he'd be more careful. From now on, he'd avoid the black-haired beauty altogether.

He watched her move into line next to Miguel. Watched her look up at the foreman with those enormous doe eyes, watched Miguel smile as if drinking her in...same as Cody. Only, Miguel had a right to look at her that way.

Oscar Duke approached the two young people and said something Cody couldn't make out. He clapped both of them on the back and laughed. Miguel smiled, and Juliana looked down at her hands.

He nearly had to summons Atlas's strength to pull his gaze away, but he finally did. Found a new place to rest his eyes as he focused on the big pots of beans and rice José and Mrs. Fuentes ladled into bowls. Focused on keeping his place in line as he followed along behind the other hired help, until finally, bowl in hand, he seated himself at one of the long tables.

"What has you so deep in thought, Ranger?" Oscar Duke took the seat across from him.

Cody scrambled for an appropriate answer. He couldn't very well tell the man that his stunning daughter had him addlepated. "I think I'll look around on my own this afternoon, if that's all right with you. I'd like to explore the Mustang Caves."

"Be careful. Those horses spook pretty easily."

"I'd also like to talk more with the sheriff. I met him earlier."

Duke nodded. "I'll send one of my men for him, see if he can meet you tomorrow."

"Sounds good to me." Cody spooned in another bite of the savory bean concoction, grateful for the chance to lasso his thoughts. Lassoing his heart...that was another story.

CHAPTER 5

"A time to rend, and a time to sew; a time to keep silence, and a time to speak."
Ecclesiastes 3:7

Juliana cut, basted, and sewed by the dim kerosene light until her eyes drooped and her back ached. That was better than lying in bed, staring at the ceiling, the handsome Ranger's image branded on her mind.

Each time his face showed up in her thoughts, she'd push it away and force thoughts of Miguel. Miguel was her future. Miguel loved her. He would cherish her and care for her all her days. Cody Steves, it seemed, would simply string her along and cast her aside.

Like today. Teasing her, singing to her. Flirting with that line in his song about a kiss. Then, *slam.* He was as absent emotionally as if he'd been clear in another county, not riding beside her on her very own property.

No. She would not waste another breath on the likes of Cody Steves.

She needed to accept the inevitable. It was her place to

marry, to produce an heir. She wasn't free to pursue her own dreams. If she did, she'd disappoint her parents, who had loved her so tenderly all her days. With her twentieth birthday approaching, the time had come.

This encounter with Cody was a good thing. It brought her heart's desires—and the insanity of those longings—to the surface. Cody carried around a guitar and sang...but it wasn't his whole life. He was a Texas Ranger. He had his job, and he saved his love for the arts as a hobby. That's what she'd do, as well. She would fulfill her duty and pass her free time with sketches and creations.

Miguel would be good to her. She'd have a long and happy life as a rancher's wife.

Although, as she snipped and sewed in the dim light, she couldn't push aside the feeling that life would be so much more pleasant if shared with someone who understood her creative spirit, rather than just allowing it. Someone who spoke the language of her heart.

A soft knock sounded at her door, followed by the sound of wood scraping against the rug as it opened. "Juliana? Why are you still awake, *bambina?*"

"Just trying a new pattern, Mama."

Mama looked at the dress pieces laid out on the floor. "Very nice. I like the brown lace over the blue fabric. I wouldn't have thought to combine the two."

"Thank you."

The older woman sat on the edge of Juliana's bed. "Tell me what's really keeping you up, my love."

Juliana gathered fabric pieces and folded them together, but didn't respond.

"I saw you talking to Miguel today."

"Miguel and I talk every day."

"Something seemed different this time."

Juliana wasn't ready to discuss her thoughts with Mama.

Once Mama knew, it was all but official. She'd have the wedding planned and the cake baked within a week.

Mama sighed. "Oh, Juliana. You have always needed to do things your own way, in your own time."

Juliana picked up stray threads from the carpet. Normally she would have left them for tomorrow, but she needed something to do with her hands. If she started talking, she'd probably burst into tears.

"This doesn't have anything to do with a nice-looking Ranger, does it?"

Juliana froze, her body stiffening like she'd been caught sneaking out the window. How could Mama know?

"Ahhh...just as I suspected. The minute I saw Lt. Steves, I had a feeling he'd catch your eye. Any woman would be blind not to notice him."

"Mama, I—"

"It's all right, sweet girl. You're not spoken for. It's only normal that you'd be curious about someone new. Just don't let a handsome stranger blind you to what's right in front of your face."

"I'm not blind, Mama. I know what's expected of me." Juliana stood, stretched her back, and flopped on the bed next to Mama.

Mama didn't speak for a few long moments. "What do you think is expected of you?"

"To marry Miguel and have a son."

Mama laughed. "You are wrong, dear girl. What is expected of you is to be happy. And if Miguel can make you happy, that's what your Papa and I want."

"And if he can't?"

"Then we don't want you to marry him. But Juliana, I've seen the way you look at the Ranger. And I've not seen him look at you the same way."

Ouch. Mama's words stung like the whip of a scorpion's tail.

"I'm sure he's noticed your beauty, but he doesn't seem to be trying to get to know you. And you deserve someone who sees what a treasure you are."

It was true. The two times they'd been alone, Cody had seemed genuinely interested in her as a person. But when they were around others, the man seemed more interested in avoiding her.

"Juliana." Mama interrupted her thoughts, her voice soft, almost a whisper.

She looked at her mother.

"Miguel is a young man...and men have...needs. Do you understand what I'm saying?"

Juliana blushed. Yes, she knew exactly what Mama meant. She did not want to have this conversation.

"He loves you. I believe you love him too, and your love for him will grow. He will be good to you, and you will be happy. It's not right to keep him waiting."

Cody's rugged face swam in Juliana's mind. But all he cared about was finding some cattle thieves. He had a job to do, then he'd be gone. She'd be foolish to waste any more time on him.

She decided to take the plunge. "Mama, I've decided to accept Miguel's offer of marriage."

The smile that stretched Mama's face lit up the dim room. The woman clapped her hands together, then hugged Juliana so tight she almost lost her breath. "I'm so happy to hear you say that! You are a wise girl. I know you and Miguel will have a wonderful life together."

CHAPTER 6

"Two are better than one, because they have a good reward for their labour."
Ecclesiastes 4:9

The next morning, Sheriff Gardner acted friendly and professional. He shared his findings and details about the case with Cody, and even offered to help however he could.

"I've had a tip that a notorious group of Mexican bandits are behind this. So far, we've been fortunate. They slaughter people as quickly as they'll slaughter an animal. If they're slipping in from the Mexican border, it'll be hard to stop them."

"Have you contacted the Mexican authorities?" Cody asked.

"The Mexican government doesn't typically cooperate with the U.S. There's still some bad blood after the battle at San Jacinto."

Cody rubbed his palm over his chin. He needed to shave. "It's been more than fifty years. You'd think they'd get over it."

Gardner laughed. "The way they see it, we stole their property right out from under them. That kind of political disaster doesn't fade quickly or quietly."

"I suppose you're right."

"We do need to get this under control. It's a big problem, not only for Duke Ranch, but for others as well. When these bandits prey on smaller ranches, they take away a family's livelihood. Duke can handle the loss better than others in these parts."

Cody looked across the acres of land. "Duke may be able to absorb the financial loss better, but stealing is stealing. Whoever is doing this needs to be caught."

The sheriff nodded. "Let's work together. I'll share any new information with you, and you do the same."

Cody nodded, pleased with how cooperative the man was being. "Sounds like a good plan."

For the next three days, Cody managed to avoid Juliana altogether, other than a glimpse here and there. He packed a lunch and set out early each morning, and returned long after dinnertime to a reheated dinner set back on the stove for him. He examined fences, talked to ranch hands, and studied the property for possible hiding places.

The best he could figure, the rustlers were holed up somewhere on the property, or just outside it. When they received word that a cattle barge was near, they could set up their next escape route. Thus far, they had covered their tracks pretty well. He hated to hope for another strike, but it looked like the best way to catch them was in the middle of the action.

Mostly, his mind stayed busy with the investigation. Sometimes, during those long, monotonous stretches of land, he strummed his guitar and sang old hymns. Every time he tried to make up a new song, all he could think of was a pair of dark brown eyes fringed with thick lashes.

Juliana.

Would she haunt his thoughts forever?

Surely he was just surprised by her beauty, and it had somehow struck a lonely chord in his soul. Atlas snorted, as if agreeing with Cody's thoughts. This was nonsense. He'd watched his friend Rett fall for his wife, Elizabeth, in the middle of a case. Though everything turned out well in the end, that lapse in Rett's judgment nearly cost lives. Cody would not make the same mistake by mooning over some pretty señorita.

Enough. He wanted to check out the Mustang Caves again. His investigation with Gardner the other day had turned up nothing. The bandits probably knew of his presence and moved around to keep from being found.

When he topped the ridge to Mustang Valley, there was Gardner. Cody waved to get the man's attention.

"There you are!" Gardner said. "I've looked all over for you. I have a lead."

"Tell me."

"A barge was spotted coming this way from the Mexican coast, off Matamoros. It should be here sometime tomorrow."

Interesting. "Won't they make their move at night?"

"Probably so. There are a lot of little coves and inlets to hide in until dark, but I feel certain when it comes, it will be from the waters off Mexico."

Made sense. "They're smart, though. They've waited for a waning moon. It'll be dark."

"Yeah, but the way the stars reflect off the water here, you should be able to see the silhouette of anything that comes near. We'll get a group of men to help us keep watch and leave early in the morning. The ride to the coast takes a few hours. I'd like you to go to the north edge."

Cody wasn't sure he wanted to be directed, but said nothing. "Where will you be?"

"I'll stay inside the fence line about a quarter of the way up, on the coast. That way I can back you up. If you miss them, maybe I can catch them."

Cody nodded. "We'll need eight or ten men, so we can post ourselves up this side of the border. Why don't we head to the ranch and make plans with the others?"

Gardner led the way back to the Duke home. Hopefully, they'd have themselves some rustlers within the next couple of days, and Cody could head home. As far from Juliana Duke as he could get.

The thought brought a wave of tightness to his chest.

They arrived to the sound of music—an interesting blend of polka and Hispanic music, with some sort of unique drum, and an interesting guitar with a large, round body. And was that an accordion?

Come to think of it, Oscar had mentioned something yesterday about a special, big dinner his wife planned. Cody had forgotten all about it.

No one else had, apparently. Everywhere, ranch hands danced with their wives and children, or scattered about tables and chairs that had been added to the lawn. From the gazebo, several men played instruments, and he longed to join them. But he didn't know any of the songs they played.

To one side of the gazebo, Juliana stood with her mother, and Cody sucked in a breath. Every time he saw her, his heart stopped for a moment, and his lungs ceased their function. She stole the breath from his body.

She wore a deep burgundy dress with gold and black trim. Around her neck hung a heart-shaped pendant, attached with a black ribbon. Her hair was scooped on top of her head, with loose black curls scattered around her neck and face.

For a moment he forgot why he'd come back early. He wanted to take her in his arms, dance with her. Maybe he'd do that after he stabled Atlas. What was the harm in a little dance?

But when he exited the barn, Oscar Duke had called for the music to stop and gathered everyone's attention. "In my opinion, any day we're all alive is a good excuse for a party." Everyone laughed. "But tonight, we have a very special announcement to make. Tonight, I'd like to announce that my daughter Juliana and Miguel, here, are officially engaged to be married."

The crowd roared. Miguel grinned like the Cheshire cat. Juliana blushed. Cody's feet turned to boulders.

Then, for an instant that felt like an eternity, her eyes met his.

CHAPTER 7

*"The heart is deceitful above all things and beyond cure Who can
understand it?"*
Jeremiah 17:9

The last few days had kept Juliana so busy, she didn't
have time to analyze her decision. She would marry
Miguel. She'd be happy. The End.

Of course, with any excuse for a party, Mama was in her
element. The louder the music, the spicier the food, the better.

So Juliana poured herself into helping Mama plan the menu
and spread the word. And of course, Mama gave her plenty of
time to sew up a new dress—something she'd sketched out
nearly a year ago, for a special occasion. Each time she'd gone
into Brownsville since then, she'd tucked a few more items into
her basket, just for that dress. The deep red taffeta fabric, the
black lace trim, the gold braiding, the black pearl-like buttons.
Slowly, she'd found everything she needed.

Her excitement for that dress overshadowed her anxiety
about making this engagement official. This was a beginning.
This was an ending. Like it or not, this was the door she was

meant to go through. Might as well keep her hand to the plow and move forward.

So that's exactly what she did. Plowed forward, keeping her hands and her mind busy until Friday evening, when the workers gathered with their families, bringing dishes to add to the big table. When the band began its warm-up, and the children danced before the party had even begun. When Mama pushed her gently toward Miguel, who gazed at her like a kitten eyeing a new ball of yarn.

"You look more beautiful than all the stars in the sky," he told her. "You always do."

"Thank you. You look very handsome, as well."

Despite the noise, they stood in awkward silence for a moment. Then another moment. This was silly. This was Miguel, whom she'd known her entire life. But somehow, things had changed. They stood like strangers during the first three or four songs.

"Would you...uh...care to dance?" he asked, when the band struck a familiar tune.

She was about to say yes when she saw Cody across the yard, headed toward the stables with Atlas. Why did he distract her so? Her heart belonged to Miguel now. Didn't it?

That's when Papa asked the musicians to stop playing and called everyone to attention. It was time. Juliana sucked in a breath and held it. No turning back now.

"We're all family here at Duke Ranch," her father said, and many people nodded. "Though we may not be joined by blood, we're joined in our hearts. And tonight, we celebrate. In my opinion, any day we're alive is an excuse for a party..." The crowd laughed and agreed. Juliana's chest clenched. She pasted a smile on her face.

At Papa's announcement about their engagement, everyone cheered. It was what they all expected, what they all had waited for. Heat rushed Juliana's face, only this didn't feel like the kind of flush she should feel at being in love. It felt more like the flush she got when she was four and told Mama she didn't know what happened to the pan dulce, while her face and fingers had been covered in sugar.

Still, she played the part the best she could, smiling and nodding at different, familiar faces in the crowd until her gaze fell on Cody, standing just outside the stables. Despite the heat, something inside her froze.

What was he thinking?

She couldn't tell. He didn't look happy at her news, but he didn't look upset, either. More like...shocked. Hurt, maybe? No. Was she reading into his expression what she wanted to be there? Mama was right. Cody Steves was *not* interested in her. And Miguel. What was she doing?

God, help my wayward heart.

The music started back up. She offered Miguel her best smile. "You were saying?"

He really was handsome. Those white teeth against that work-earned tan...broad shoulders and a slim waist. When did the boy she knew become a man? What woman wouldn't melt at the sight of him?

"I was asking if you'd like to dance." He bowed slightly, and she couldn't help but giggle. Miguel? Being a grown-up gentleman, treating her like a grown-up lady? It was preposterous. It was delightful.

"I'd love to, Señor Fuentes."

With that, Miguel whisked her onto the makeshift dance floor. Those nearby stepped back to make room for them. The crowd cheered and clapped, and for three numbers they danced and laughed until Juliana was out of breath. Yes, life with Miguel would be fun. And sweet. Even if he didn't make her heart sizzle with romance like Mama's spicy chili, so what? Chili gave her heartburn.

"Would you care for some punch?" Miguel asked her.

"Yes, please. I'm parched."

She watched him make his way through the crowd toward Mama's punch bowl, where he stopped and spoke to Emily Gardner. Juliana would have to make time to talk to her this evening. They'd once been best of friends, but lately...

Miguel moved on again, weaving through the crush until Sheriff Gardner and Cody stopped him. She looked away. Best to find someplace else to rest her eyes.

"Congratulations." Emily approached from the shadows.

"Thank you. I'm glad you came."

"Yes, well. It's not every day I get invited to a party." Did Emily's smile lack sincerity?

"That's a lovely dress. Where did you get it?" For the last year or more, Juliana had tried to draw the sheriff's daughter into the types of conversations they shared when they were younger. But something in Emily shut off, and Juliana didn't know how to get it back.

"I ordered it from a catalogue."

"Oh. Well, it's quite becoming on you." The exchange slipped toward a painful, awkward death. Should Juliana try to revive it again? Walk away, and give it a mercy killing? "Have you tried the punch? Mama makes delicious punch."

"No."

Gracious and mercy. If Emily didn't want to talk, why did she approach? "What a lovely scent. Is that your perfume?"

"It's called Heliotrope."

Juliana followed Emily's gaze to land on Miguel. She was acting odd, even for her. "It reminds me of almonds and cherries, and maybe some vanilla?"

Emily responded with another strained smile, but said nothing.

"Well, I'd better see if Mama needs anything. Thank you again for coming."

Cody wanted nothing more than to make himself scarce. Unfortunately, he and Sheriff Gardner needed to talk to Miguel and Mr. Duke. Come to think of it, with all the men together like this, it might be the perfect time to set up plans for tomorrow.

He skirted the perimeter of the party and tried not to watch the couple of honor dance the night away. He consumed three cups of punch, four tortillas filled with beans and rice, and several little rolls of sweet bread before he heard Gardner clap someone on the back, directly to his left.

"Miguel, my boy. Congratulations and best wishes. You've got yourself a pretty little filly, there."

"Thank you, sir." Miguel sounded out of breath.

"I hate to talk business right now, but the Ranger and I made some plans, and we're gonna need your help."

"I...was just about to bring Juliana some punch. She's thirsty. But—"

"Nonsense. The Ranger will be more than happy to deliver that punch to your gal, won't you, Lieutenant?" Gardner poured the punch himself and handed it to Cody. "I'll fill Miguel in until you get back."

Cody took the cup, mostly because he wasn't ready to face Miguel. Then he'd have to congratulate him. "I'll be right back." He nudged his way through the crowd, toward Juliana, who stood near her mother.

With each step, tension grew like a boa constrictor around his gut. He wanted to be near her, yet wanted to get as far from her as he could. It was a torturous form of madness he'd developed since he'd first laid eyes on her a few days ago.

He offered her the punch. "Miguel said you were thirsty. He was detained by Sheriff Gardner."

She took it and studied the cup's contents as if it were the most interesting thing in the room. "Thank you."

"You're welcome." He should leave. Now.

"You should play with the band."

"I don't know these songs."

Her gaze met his, stealing his breath. "I'm sure you'd catch on easily enough."

He really should go.

"Why don't I introduce you to the band leader?" She motioned toward an older man. "Pedro! Come here. I'd like to introduce you to Lt. Steves. He plays the guitar."

The gray-haired man shook Cody's hand. "*Encantado.* Pleased to meet you. You have your guitar with you?"

"It's upstairs in my room."

"Then you must get it and play with us. You wouldn't want to disappoint the lady on such a special night, would you?"

Uh... "No. I wouldn't."

Pedro smiled and turned back to where his fellow instrumentalists took a break.

Cody turned back to Juliana. He should really say something...like... "I'm happy for you."

She studied her punch again, swirling the liquid in the cup. "Thank you. That's kind of you to say."

"I...can see Miguel loves you. I hope the two of you will be...happy." How many more times could he use the word happy before the conversation ended?

"Juliana! There you are, my love." Mrs. Duke appeared through the crowd. "*Hola,* Lt. Steves. May I borrow my daughter for a moment?"

"Certainly. I was just—" The women walked away before he could finish his sentence.

Might as well do as he was told and get his guitar. Although his job was to catch cattle rustlers, he knew the wisdom in keeping his very wealthy host happy. And there was that word again. If everyone around him was so happy, why did he feel like he wanted to punch something?

With focused precision, Cody slipped his way through the crowd, into the house, and to his room. Grabbed his guitar and headed for the back stairway—the servants' stairway, though he'd been given permission to use the grand front entrance. This way was faster.

When he reached the bottom step leading to the kitchen doorway, he nearly collided with Juliana. They stood there, suspended in time, her face inches from his in the dim light. He could smell her perfume. If he wanted, he could kiss her right now. Where did that thought come from?

"Oh! *Lo siento*. I'm sorry."

"My fault. I should have paid more attention."

An electrical charge filled the space. Did she feel it too? One look at her flushed cheeks, her dilated pupils... She felt it.

"Lt. Steves..." Her voice was husky.

"Yes?" The word came out in a whisper, though he didn't plan it that way.

"I..." She looked from his eyes to his lips. She leaned in.

His body acted without his brain telling it to. He leaned into her, and their lips met. Just barely met, in a soft, slow brush of a kiss that sent his heart rate soaring. One hand still held his guitar case, but he reached his other around her waist.

Her arms came around his neck, and the kiss deepened, her lips full and warm on his. It was the most delicious thing he'd ever tasted.

Slowly, hesitantly, they pulled back, like two magnets being forced apart against the laws of nature. Neither spoke for a too-long moment.

Oh, man. What had he just done?

As if having the same question, she stepped back, as far against the wall as she could in the small space. "I..."

"I'm sorry, Juliana. Miss Duke, I mean. That should have never happened."

"It...it's not your fault. I did it too."

Cody backed up one step, moved to the opposite side so she could pass. When she moved forward, she looked up at him, her eyes scared, confused.

"Miss Duke, I won't tell anyone what just happened here. You have my word."

"I...thank you." She dipped her head, moved past him, and continued up the stairs.

He watched her retreat, his heart holding a wrestling match of longing and regret. After a moment, he tightened his grip on his guitar case and went in search of Pedro.

CHAPTER 8

"A time to weep, and a time to laugh; a time to mourn and a time to dance."
Ecclesiastes 3:4

The remainder of the evening was surreal. Juliana danced nearly every dance with Miguel, saving a few for Papa. She should have felt beautiful and grown-up. Should have lavished in the attention everyone gave her. Instead, she felt certain she'd toss her tortillas at any moment.

What had she been thinking? She had never been so forward with any man. Certainly not with Miguel. What was it about Cody Steves that caused her brain to turn to pudding?

Did he kiss her, or did she kiss him? She wasn't sure. One thing she did know, though. They *both* participated. They *both* enjoyed it, however brief the moment.

She was such a cad! A ghastly beast, was what she was. Did this make her an adulteress?

No. She wasn't married.

A fallen woman?

She hoped not. The fact that she *liked* the kiss so much left her wondering.

With all her might, she heaved her thoughts away from the Ranger and the kiss to a more appropriate topic—the only topic that could crowd her mind from top to bottom.

Dress design.

She'd be designing a wedding gown soon. She knew Papa would spare no expense for the fabric and supplies—she could have anything she wanted. As she pieced together the dress in her mind, she momentarily forgot her resolve not to look at the gazebo, where Cody had taken his place with the band.

But when her eyes accidentally fell on him, strumming his guitar and looking for all the world like he belonged here, on their ranch, she pictured him standing opposite her at the altar. What was wrong with her?

She knew better. Mama would say, *Querer estar en Misa y en procession*, or, *You wish to be at Mass and in the procession.*

Papa would say, *You can't have your cake and eat it too.*

Problem was, she wasn't sure she wanted the cake named Miguel. She wanted a different flavor, entirely. What a wicked, wicked heart she had. *Ah, Dios! I want to love Miguel. I really do. What is wrong with me, Lord?*

She had let a handsome cowboy turn her brain upside down, and now she'd agreed to something she wasn't ready to agree to simply because...

She didn't know why.

Why couldn't the Rangers have sent some old, stodgy, cigar-smoking fellow with tobacco breath and a pooch belly? Who *couldn't* sing.

Miguel pulled her close and whispered in her ear. "It's been a beautiful night, Juliana. Hopefully the first of many to come. I look forward to growing old with you."

Juliana wanted to cry. But she mustered the right words. "Yes. Me too." She was the worst kind of villain.

~

"*R*anger!" Miguel called to Cody during a break in the music.

Cody stiffened. Did he know? Had he seen? "Yes?"

"When the party ends, Mr. Duke wants all the men together to make plans for tomorrow evening. Right here, in the courtyard."

Cody grasped his composure and slowly released the long breath he'd held. "I'll be right here." Then he shoved the last hour from his mind and tried to let music consume his thoughts. It wasn't every day he got to learn a whole new style of playing.

The technique was fascinating, really. The difference in this unique style lay not so much in the actual chords—those were pretty much the same in any type of music—but in the rhythms and strumming patterns. Down-up with the thumb, down with the fingers, up-down with thumb, slap the strings with his palm. He'd never heard anything like it before.

He poured all his concentration into learning the intricacies of this unique way of playing. It opened up a whole new world of songs for him. Before long, he'd pushed the raven-haired beauty to the back of his brain as he became absorbed in the joy of his craft.

Almost. Once, he caught her eye while she danced with Miguel. Cody quickly looked away. He kept his eyes close to his instrument, or on his bandmates, the rest of the evening.

He played back-up to the accordion, which took the lead. The large drum, called a ranch drum, pounded out the low, succinct rhythm. And that strange guitar, with so many strings! He was dying to get his hands on it. How did that player handle all those strings with such control?

Eventually the twilight gave way to starlight. Candles and

lanterns hung here and there, flickering in the soft wind, and the music was a soothing balm to his frustrated heart.

When he'd strummed the last chord of the final song, the other musicians laughed and clapped him on the back, shook his hand and told him "well done." Would they be so accommodating if they knew *what* he'd done?

They spent a few minutes showing him their instruments, and each of them tried out his guitar. He learned the strange guitar was called an oajo sexton, and the music style was called "conjunto," or collection. It was a blend of music from northern Mexico and some different immigrant groups in Texas, including German and Czech. Despite the evening's rocky start, he ended up enjoying himself.

Now, back to work.

As he placed his guitar in the soft leather case he'd created especially for travelling, he felt, more than saw, someone looking at him. A turn of his head confirmed it.

Juliana.

Deep breath, Cody. A few more days, and you'll be out of here. Hopefully. "Nice party."

"You looked like you were having fun up here."

"These fellows can really play." Didn't she have something better to do besides look at him with those eyes he could so easily drown in? Hadn't she tortured him enough for one evening?

"Yes. Mama makes sure they have plenty of opportunities to perform. She loves to throw parties."

"Maybe so. But it's not every day she gets to throw one like this."

Juliana looked away, and a northeast wind played with her curls, with the ribbons on her dress. "I suppose that's true." Her brow furrowed, and the tiny lines around her lips tightened.

She didn't look like a woman in love. More like a woman in distress. Was she trying not to cry?

Cody pressed back the urge to question her. It wasn't his place. Best keep as much distance between them as possible. He tied the guitar securely into its pouch and slung the instrument over his shoulder. "Miss Duke, it's been a delight. But I have to get back to work. If you'll excuse me."

"Yes, of course. Thank you for...for playing tonight."

"My pleasure." He walked past her toward the tables where the men congregated, while the women gathered their dishes and helped clean up. He refused to hesitate, refused to look back.

But something in his spirit wondered just what would become of Miss Juliana Duke. And if his heart would ever be the same, after knowing her for only a few short days.

～

Juliana swam against the current of her swirling thoughts and tried to find shore. Right now, there was a lot of clean up to do. Best stay busy with a task. She picked up several plates and stacked them on her arm like Mama had taught her.

"No, no, chiquita! You are the guest of honor. Tonight is your night. Relax. Go upstairs, hang up your pretty dress, and dream about Miguel." Mama took the plates from her.

"I want to help. I'm so wound up, I probably won't sleep anyway."

Mama laughed. "Ah, to be young and in love. Suit yourself." She handed the plates back. "So you had fun tonight? The fiesta was everything you hoped for?"

How was she supposed to answer that? "As always, you outdid yourself, Mama. Thank you."

Mama took the plates again and set them on the table. "Sit down."

Juliana obeyed, and Mama sat beside her. "Your mouth

smiles, but your eyes do not. Tell me what is going on in your pretty head."

"Nothing, Mama. It's just been a long day."

Mama looked at her like she was studying a new recipe and didn't have all the ingredients. Then she shifted her gaze to the group of men on the opposite side of the pavilion. "Is your heart torn, *cariño?*"

"Mama, no." That was a lie. "I...don't try to read things that aren't there. I'm happy." She didn't sound happy at all. She was the worst liar in the world. "Miguel is great. He's handsome, kind, smart. What girl wouldn't be thrilled to have him?" At least that was all truth.

"Maybe I pushed you. I did. I pushed you." Mama put her face in her hands.

"Mama, no. I'm fine. See?" She found her best smile and worked hard to make it go to her eyes. "I'm just tired, but I'm also wound up. If you'll let me get back to cleaning this mess, it'll probably wear me out enough so I can sleep."

"Are you sure?"

"I'm sure." She kissed her mother on top of her gray-streaked hair, grabbed the stack of plates, and whisked away before Mama could say more.

~

Cody sat on one of the wooden benches and leaned against the table behind him. Sheriff Gardner directed the men like this was his operation, and Cody was just one of the hired hands. So be it. Challenging the man's authority in a public setting would bring no good.

Something about the man didn't quite settle with Cody. It was probably just the sting of being treated like a subordinate, when he was no such thing. Still, Cody listened to the sheriff's plans for tomorrow morning's stake-out and made mental notes about who was to go where and when.

"The Duke property covers hundreds of miles. If we're going to catch these rustlers, we have to spread out. Duke, how many men can you spare in the morning?"

"I can give you twenty." Mr. Duke started calling names of the ranch hands he could spare.

Gardner began pairing them off. Cody tried not to look at Juliana, gathering dishes from a table to his left. His attention yanked back when he heard his name. "Lt. Steves, you and Miguel will head southwest and cover the land between the south peninsula and the cove."

Miguel? Great.

Mr. Duke stood, effectively taking the floor from Gardner. "I'd like to hear what the Ranger has to add to these plans."

Cody didn't look at Gardner, but sensed something like resentment from the man. "I think the sheriff has a good plan. As we ride our assigned areas, don't just look for evidence of human disturbance. These guys are smart enough to cover their tracks. Also look for places any large structure can hide. There's a chance they're hiding the barge in some brush right on the property. Also remember that if our hunch is correct and they're stealing cattle on the shore, those cattle must be able to get onto the barge. Land that's too marshy or boggy is out."

"Good points, Lt." Gardner moved next to Mr. Duke, taking control again. "Gentlemen, you have an early morning. Meet here at five a.m. and be ready to leave at first light."

The men shuffled away in groups of two and three, discussing their thoughts on the plan of action. At least, Cody assumed that's what they discussed, since many of them spoke in Spanish.

Cody pushed to his feet, replaced his hat on his head, and grabbed his guitar. He felt, more than saw, Miguel's eyes on him. Cody met the man's gaze, but neither of them spoke. Instead, they each nodded and walked in opposite directions.

He pushed down the nausea that roiled in his gut. Gardner may be a questionable character, but Miguel seemed solid and sincere. Which made what happened earlier tonight even more despicable.

CHAPTER 9

"Delight yourself in the Lord, and He will give you the desires of your heart."
Psalm 37:4

*D*espite lying awake until the wee hours of the morning, Juliana awoke at five a.m. When she heard the sheriff partner Miguel and Cody the night before, she nearly dropped the heirloom serving bowl she held. Those two alone for hours? Would they talk about her?

Would Cody tell Miguel what happened?

No. He promised, and he was a man of his word.

She hoped.

She threw back the covers and padded to her window. Opened the latch. If she leaned forward and looked to the left, she might catch a glimpse of the men as they prepared to leave. Sure enough, lantern light flooded the pavilion like a halo. Voices drifted her way, but she couldn't make out the words.

Slowly, softly, she shut the window and replaced the latch. What did she hope to see? To hear?

Cody. She wanted to see Cody. Guilt pulsed and throbbed

with every beat of her heart. *I'm acting like a child who's given a beautiful Christmas present, only to envy my cousin's gift because it's different.* Miguel was indeed a gift. Loyal, kind, intelligent, handsome. Well, no more of this nonsense. Today, she'd stop acting like a child and be the chaste, virtuous young woman she'd been taught to be.

Every time she thought of Cody, she'd say Miguel's name out loud. Five times.

Cody. "Miguel-Miguel-Miguel-Miguel-Miguel!"

Okay, maybe ten times. Good heavens. So much for being mature.

She turned up the lantern by her bed, picked up her Bible, and crawled back under the covers. Didn't open it. Just held it there, close to her heart. "God? What is wrong with me?" she whispered into the quiet room. Saying her prayers out loud made it feel more like a real conversation.

"A few weeks ago, God, I wasn't satisfied with my life. I wanted something to change. Now I have all these changes. Cody has come. Miguel and I are engaged. And I'm even less satisfied." A single tear made its way down her cheek, to her chin, and she brushed it away.

"I know Cody can't *possibly* be the man for me. He's a Ranger, for goodness' sake. He'll probably never settle down. Why am I so drawn to him?" More tears. She clutched the Bible to her chest and nestled beneath the covers.

"And here's Miguel, ready to love me more than any woman has a right to be loved. And I betray him on the night our engagement is announced? God, everything is so mixed up."

When she stopped talking to God, she didn't know. But somewhere, in that place between awake and asleep, her favorite scripture drifted through her mind. *Delight yourself in the Lord, and He will give you the desires of your heart.*

~

"*W*hat led you to join the Rangers?"

Miguel and Cody had ridden over an hour without more than a grunt or two. Now he wanted to talk? "I dunno. Lots of things, I guess. My uncle was a sheriff's deputy, and I always admired him. My parents and I lived on a remote farm, and the Rangers came through from time to time. Mom would invite them to supper. Sometimes they'd stay the night. My older brother inherited the farm, and I became a lawman."

They rode a while longer before Miguel responded. Funny how, this close to the water, there were patches that felt like desert, blanketed with sand and rock, dotted with cactus. Cody checked his compass to make sure they were still headed the right direction. A tiny stream—more a trickle, really, meandered over the rocky soil. Yeah, they were going the right way.

Miguel drew up beside him, let his horse, Sal, lap from the water. Atlas followed suit. "It must be nice to have a choice in what you'll do with your life."

"You don't have a choice?" Cody adjusted his hat to block the early morning sun.

"I...suppose I do. And to be honest, ranching is in my blood. But if I were to choose any other path, I'd disappoint a lot of people."

"I guess that's true." Why was Miguel sharing all this? The last thing he wanted was to become the man's buddy. *Miguel* was too hard to say. Mike? What would he do if Cody called him Mickey? He pulled his thoughts back to their current mission. "What can you tell me about the Mustang Caves?"

"What would you like to know?"

"It seems to me, they'd be a great place for rustlers to hide."

"The sheriff rides that area regularly. He likes the view, and he and Mr. Duke are old friends. Duke gives him free rein on the property. Gardner would know if anything odd happened down there."

Cody didn't like the path his thoughts took. "I guess that's true." Apparently, he was short on vocabulary this morning. Atlas whinnied as if in agreement. Cody clicked his tongue, signaling the horse to move again.

"I guess it wouldn't hurt to check things out." Miguel clicked, and Sal kept pace with Atlas. "I can take you down there sometime."

Cody almost told him Juliana already had, but he choked back the words. He refused to bring Juliana into any conversation with Miguel.

"Juliana is something special, isn't she?"

And there it was. "You're a lucky man."

"Do you have anybody special waiting for you?"

What kind of question was that? What kind of man asked that of another man? He looked at Miguel, and there he saw it. Uncertainty? Jealousy?

"Being a Ranger doesn't exactly lend itself to settling down."

"Aww, come on. There's gotta be some married Rangers."

Yes. Yes, there were. He thought of Rett and Elizabeth Smith. They seemed pretty happy. Okay, deliriously happy. Except when Rett went out on assignment, and Elizabeth walked around town with a smile on her face and anxiety in her eyes. Others may not see it, but Cody did. "A few." How could he get out of this conversation?

Miguel drew up Sal in front of Atlas, forcing them both to a stop. "My whole life, I've known Juliana was the girl for me. If anyone ever tried to stand in my way, I don't know what might happen."

Was that a threat? "Well, it seems you have an entire community cheering on your relationship. I'm sure no one would dream of coming between you."

"I hope not." Miguel spurred Sal into a trot and left Cody in his dust.

Good. Now that he'd got that out of his system, maybe

Miguel would shut up and start tracking some rustlers. This was exactly why Cody liked to work alone.

~

The sun was high in the sky when Juliana stirred from the deepest sleep she'd had in weeks. She pushed the covers back for the second time that day and slipped out of bed.

Somehow, while she slept, her heart had come to a more settled place. Cody Steves was an infatuation and nothing more. Of course she'd be drawn to a handsome stranger who shared so many common interests. Cody was like one of those penny stories in the ladies' magazines. Exciting to read, but soon his chapter in her life would end.

Miguel. He would stay. He would love her all her days. Theirs might not be a spicy romance, but it would be sweet. How many times had Mama told her love was not a feeling? It was a decision. She decided to love Miguel, and that was that.

She opened the door to her wardrobe and selected one of three green dresses. Miguel's favorite color. From now on, every decision would be made to please him.

When would the men return? She'd stay close to the house, to make sure she was around when he got back. She grabbed her drawing supplies and headed for the veranda. But first, the kitchen. She was starved, and she smelled bacon.

CHAPTER 10

"The voice of the Lord is upon the waters; the God of glory thundereth."
Psalm 29:3

The afternoon sun beat mercilessly from both the sky and the water from a little cove—the farthest point on the map they'd been given. Six hours of riding, and they were maybe ten or twelve miles from the house. They'd found nothing along the way, and now there was only a bunch of seaweed and salt spray on one side, bordered by thick hackberry brush, Texas persimmon, and some live oaks.

No cattle prints. No evidence that anyone had been here in, well, ever. Cody and Miguel continued along the coastline, looking for anything to report. Hopefully the others had better luck.

He had some questions for Miguel, but he needed to tread lightly. Cattlemen were an odd breed. Fierce loyalty to their own, and they'd tear up an outsider quicker than a starved pack of coyotes if you crossed them. "You say Duke and Gardner have been friends a while, eh?"

"Since they were kids. Gardner's father was a cattleman in this area. He owned the land adjacent to Duke on the north east. He and the Senior Mr. Duke worked side by side."

"Oh? He's no longer in the cattle business?"

"No. I'm not sure what happened. I know Gardener's father moved up north somewhere, but the sheriff decided to stay. This area is home for him."

"Does he still own land in the area?"

"Just a house in Brownsville. Duke bought the property when Mr. Gardener moved. Gave him more than its value. Wanted to make sure the man had plenty to live on."

Cody rode as he listened, trying to piece together anything that might turn into a clue. Something to his left caught his eye. "What's that?" He slid off Atlas and moved toward some brush. Bright red paint peeked through a pile of seaweed and ocean rock. He pulled at the brush, tossing it aside. Some of it was tangled, so Cody pulled his knife from its sheath at his belt. Soon, he and Miguel uncovered a small skiff. Two oars were attached with rope to rings on either side.

"Ay, *caramba!*" Miguel picked up one of the oars. "It looks like this place isn't as abandoned as I thought it was."

"It's been here a while. I don't think it belongs to our rustlers." Cody dusted sand and seaweed off his vest.

"I wonder if Mr. Duke knows it's here."

"The paint's pretty old. But the wood looks solid."

Miguel grinned like a kid in a schoolyard. "We should test it out. See if it works. Just in case we need to know, for evidence."

Cody laughed. He didn't want to like this guy. But if it weren't for Juliana, Cody could be friends with Miguel. He really was a likable fellow. "Evidence, you say?"

In no time, the two men had pulled off their boots and hats and left them, along with Cody's pack, on the shore, then dragged the skiff to the water's edge. Cody climbed in front, while Miguel pushed off and jumped in the back. There they were, two grown men, whooping and hollering as the fresh sea breeze hit their faces.

They'd rowed a few hundred feet from shore and were just turning around when a gunshot fired. From their place in the water, they watched both horses rear and bolt. Why hadn't they tethered them?

"Get down!" Cody drew his gun and lowered himself as much as he could. But the current pushed them farther out to sea, and they couldn't very well paddle from that position. Another gunshot. A bullet whizzed over their heads. "Can you swim?"

"Like a fish," Miguel answered.

"We need to get out of this boat and use it as a shield." Both men slid into the water, holding their pistols above their heads to keep them from getting wet.

More gunshots, but Cody couldn't see anyone on shore. He wasn't exactly in a position to get a good look. Cody and Miguel shot blindly toward land, into the brush. *Atlas, buddy, I hope you're out of the way.*

The next minutes passed, thick and heavy, like an invisible fog smothering the peace from moments before. Finally, the gunfire ceased. After another ten-minute eternity, the two men touched bottom and pushed the boat ashore.

With wary caution, they stayed close to the ground and moved quickly behind a pile of rocks. From that vantage point, they searched for movement farther back, behind the trees and brush.

"I think they're gone." Miguel's voice cut through the breeze.

"Yeah. So are our horses." Cody stood up, looked around, and trudged through the sand to retrieve his boots and hat, leaving a dripping trail of salt water behind him. At least he had his pack. "Guess we better start walking."

Thunder rolled in the distance. A couple of miles offshore, a storm mocked them. The wind picked up, and the hairs on Cody's arm prickled.

Miguel's brow furrowed. "We need to find cover. Now."

Cody looked around for something—anything—they could use for shelter in the storm. The trees that had appeared stately and strong when they arrived now bent and bowed with the squall. To his left, he saw a cave—more of an overhang, really. "This way!"

They ran, full speed toward the rock cavity, but Cody slowed when he saw hoofprints. Stopped.

"Hurry! It's coming fast." Miguel shouted over the roaring gusts.

"Go on. I'll be right behind you." Cody knelt down, studied the impacted ground, and tried to memorize the print. The horseshoe wasn't Atlas's. He'd have to study Sal—if they found him. The print had a v-shaped nick in it with a little curl to the left, in the upper right curve. Thunder boomed, and lighting struck a few yards from him. He had to move. Now.

Cody reached shelter a breath before the heavens dumped a dense curtain of rain behind him. Lightning taunted them just yards from where they stood. They were safe for now—barely. But one thing was certain—there would be no more hoof prints to study, once this downpour was over.

~

Juliana spent the better part of the day on the veranda designing dresses, in all sizes, shapes, and patterns. Every time her mind wandered to Cody, to that slow, delicious kiss on the stairway, she forced her thoughts to her task. To sewing.

What would it be like to own a dress shop? Something affordable. She saw the other ladies look at her with longing whenever she wore a new dress. Wasn't it every woman's right to have a new garment now and again, to feel beautiful, to feel like the belle of the ball?

Maybe not her *right*. But certainly her desire. If only she lived in a metropolitan area...but she didn't. She never would. But she did have women right here on the ranch she could sew for. If only she could get their measurements.

What if she just made a few dresses in a variety of sizes, and let the ladies choose? That's how she'd do it in a dress shop. She'd have a variety of attractive, ready-made dresses, with easy-to alter seams customers could take in or let out. That would keep costs down. There were plenty of high-end dress shops. No need to add another business to cater to that set.

Silly dreams. She watched Miguel's nieces—Isabel and Luisa—skip past the garden toward the stables. Luisa would look so pretty in lilac gingham. And Isabel...yellow would bring out her soft brown eyes. What kind of eyes would Cody's children have?

Where did that thought come from? *Stop it, Juliana.*

She watched the girls for several minutes and tried to estimate their sizes.

Thunder rolled in the distance, and lightning flashed through the sky. The pages of Juliana's sketch book fluttered in a gust of wind, and she scrambled to gather her pencils and loose pages. Cody and Miguel were out in this. And the other men too.

But they were smart enough to take cover. She pushed down the concern that pulsed through her gut.

The girls continued their giggles and games in the open field.

"Girls. A storm is coming. Andalé!"

The girls stopped but didn't move toward her. "The wind feels nice."

"I know. But it's lightning. Come inside with me. I have a surprise for you."

The disappointment in their faces turned to smiles, and they followed her through the veranda and into the kitchen, where Juanita—the girls' mother—worked.

"I'm kidnapping them to my room for a while, if that's all right with you."

Juanita dragged her gaze from the window, worry etching her eyes. "Yes, thank you. I'm sure they'll love spending time with you." She looked at the girls. "You be good for Miss Juliana, okay?"

"Yes, ma'am."

Another boom of thunder crashed, and the girls squealed, then giggled. Juliana caught Juanita's eye in shared concern. "They'll be fine," Juliana whispered.

"I know." Juanita returned to the chopping block and sliced through a pile of okra.

"Follow me." The girls held hands and skipped ahead of her to the stairs. They knew their way around the house, as they'd helped their mother with chores.

When they entered her room, Luisa grabbed Juliana's hand. "Are you going to marry my uncle?"

Goodness. She didn't want to talk about that right now. "He asked, and I said yes."

Isabel snickered.

"All the girls like Uncle Miguel." Luisa giggled behind her hands.

"Really? Like whom?" Juliana couldn't recall seeing Miguel with any of the local girls.

"Oh, there are plenty." Luisa held up her fingers like she'd count off a list.

"Be quiet!" Isabel told her sister. "You know Juliana is the one he's supposed to marry."

Supposed to marry? "I need your help with a project." Juliana swept open her dresser drawer to reveal a stack of fabric. "Will you each choose your favorite?"

Subject changed, the girls oohed and ahhed over each piece

as they held them to their faces and ran their fingers over each surface.

Today, they'd help her realize a small part of her dream. More importantly, they'd keep her mind busy while she waited for the men she cared about—two of them in particular—to return unharmed.

~

Cody and Miguel scooted as far back against the rock as they could. Rain splashed onto their already-wet clothes. At least they were protected from lightning. Neither spoke. They would have to yell over the noise. But Cody's mind raced with the events of the last hour.

Who shot at them? Was it the rustlers? Someone else?

Was Atlas all right? Would they find their horses, or have to walk back?

It took six hours to get here on horseback, but they were taking their time, looking for tracks, for clues. They could probably make it back on foot in the same amount of time.

If it ever stopped raining. But they'd be walking through mud, which would slow them down, and leave some pretty deep tracks of their own. It would be well past dark before they arrived.

Cody did a good bit of praying in that storm. Praying for their safety. Praying they'd find whoever did this. Praying they'd find the rustlers. Were they one and the same? And praying he'd be able to walk away from Miss Juliana Duke with his heart intact. He'd often wondered if that's why God brought the storms—to keep people on their knees.

After the better part of an hour, the rain slowed. Miguel uttered a few Spanish words under his breath.

"I don't know what you said, but I'm pretty sure I agree with it."

"I said, I guess we better start walking."

Cody whistled, hoping Atlas would appear, but the wind carried the sound out to sea. He stood up, dusted more dirt off his soaked jeans. "Let's go."

When they hit the soppy sand, they sank ankle deep. Cody stepped right out of his boots, and Miguel did the same.

Great.

They each tugged their boots out of the mire, hoisted one under each arm, and kept walking. At this rate, they might get back a week from Tuesday.

Between the beach and the trail lay a rocky path. Slick as ice now. Even slicker in their socks.

Two feet from the trail, Miguel slipped. Cody reached for him, but it was too late.

Miguel cried out as he sprawled on the ground, his foot caught between two rocks, his ankle bent at an unnatural angle. Blood oozed where a jagged cut from a rock zigged along the flesh. *No!*

Can it get any worse, God?

Don't answer that. Maybe they'd get back a week from *Thursday.*

Cody knelt beside Miguel for a closer look. The man was breathing hard, his face contorted. A glance at the ankle made Cody's belly churn. Nasty wound. Nastier break. "I'll need to set it."

"I know." Miguel gritted his teeth against the pain.

Cody plopped to a sitting position in the mud—no point trying to stay clean—and dug through his pack. The bottle of whiskey had been with him for two years, still unopened. It was a staple in a Ranger's supplies, for times like this. He twisted the cork and held out the container. "For the pain."

Miguel looked at it long and hard, like taking a swallow might make him seem less of a man.

"Drink it. Trust me, you'll be glad you did."

After a moment, Miguel grabbed the bottle, took a swig. Short at first. But then he tipped the bottle back and drained nearly half the contents.

"Whoa, there, amigo. Save some for later. We've got a long journey ahead." Cody took the bottle, recorked it, and set it out of reach. Took his hat to the ocean's edge and filled it with salt water. He'd clean the wound as best he could, then douse it with some whiskey. His body stung just thinking about it.

"This is gonna burn."

Miguel winced when Cody poured the cool, salty liquid. Hopefully, the salt would keep infection from settling. When he sanitized the lesion with the whiskey, Miguel let out a yelp that rivaled a coon dog in a bear trap, then uttered a string of Spanish words. Cody was pretty sure the man wasn't reciting the twenty-third Psalm.

He looked around for a sturdy stick, and maybe some seaweed to use as a wrap. He took more time than he needed, to give the whiskey a chance to numb Miguel's senses. They'd have to camp here. Under good conditions, Cody *might* be able to carry Miguel. In this soppy mess? Definitely not. He could hike back for help, but with Miguel in the shape he was, a cougar might decide he'd make a nice snack.

If Cody could find some dry wood, he could build a fire back under their rock shelter. His pack contained some hard tack and jerky. Tomorrow, maybe Atlas would show up.

"Okay, friend. I need you to bite down hard on this stick. This might hurt a little."

Miguel did as he was told, groaning only a bit when Cody snapped the bone into place. The seaweed stretched and cracked, but he kept winding it until it held the makeshift splint in place. This would have to do for now.

Could he carry Miguel back to the shelter? He might slip on the rocks and injure him worse. What could he use for a travois?

"Don't worry about me. I can crawl." Miguel laughed like he'd said something hilarious.

Good. He was too drunk to feel pain.

"All right. But let me help you." Inch by inch, Miguel dragged himself across the rocks to the sand.

At that point, Cody grabbed the other man under each arm and tugged him the rest of the way, Miguel whooping like he was on a carnival ride. At least he was a happy drunk. "You having fun, buddy?"

"Fun? I always have fun. Fun is what I do." His words slurred, and he laughed some more. "I had fun at the party last night. Did you have fun?"

"Uh... sure."

Miguel reached in his pocket, pulled out a lacy cloth, and wiped his sweat-beaded forehead.

"Nice handkerchief. I didn't take you for the frilly type, but to each his own." Cody settled the man back under the shelter and looked around for firewood. Everything was soaked.

"Oh, this. Yeah." He stuffed the cloth back into his pocket.

"Juliana give you that?"

"Yeah. Juliana."

Cody did not want to discuss Juliana. Why did he bring her up? Although, he could probably confess everything, and Miguel wouldn't remember a word of it.

Cody looked at the soft, lacy cloth sticking out of Miguel's pocket and thought of last night's soft, lacy kiss. He sure hoped Miguel fell asleep soon. He didn't need to spend hours talking about the very woman he wanted to forget.

CHAPTER 11

"Deliver the poor and needy: rid them out of the hand of the wicked."
Psalm 82:3

It was still light out when the rain stopped. A couple hours later, the men trickled in two by two, soggy and gray like they'd lived through Noah's flood. Juliana stood near the door with the other women, offering blankets and hot coffee and fresh tortillas filled with hot beans and rice. The sky darkened, but no sign of Cody or Miguel.

"He'll be here. Don't worry, my love," Mama whispered.

But then, an hour after all the other men were dry and accounted for, Juliana heard hoof beats. Her heart sped up as Cody's, then Miguel's faces filled her mind. *Miguel.* She forced his face, his voice, his essence to consume her thoughts. Tried, once again, to erase last night's kiss from her memory.

She grabbed another blanket and trotted toward the sound. In the dim light she could just make out two…horses?

Atlas and Sal. But they carried no riders. "Mama!" Her heart in her throat, she dropped the blanket and ran toward the house. "Mama. Something has happened."

"What is it, chica?"

"The Ranger and Miguel aren't back, but their horses are." Juliana fought to form the words. Their implication choked her, suffocated her with fear.

Papa approached, a group of the men right behind him. "What's this?"

Juliana pointed into the dark, where the horses neighed and whinnied. "Something's happened."

The room exploded with conversation. In English. In Spanish. Everyone at once. Her father directed a couple of men to gather the horses and take them to the barn.

After several minutes of debate that did nothing to alleviate anyone's anxiety or grief, Papa raised his voice above the others. "It's already dark. There's no point in sending out a search party now. There's too much chance of injury over the rocks, and the night's warm enough those two should be fine until morning. You all try to get some rest. Men, meet here at first light. We'll spread out in the direction they were headed, see what we can find."

The group stood around, shaking their heads and whispering concerns. Juliana couldn't accept waiting until morning. How could they just leave them out there all night? What if they were hurt? Bleeding? Cold and wet?

What if they died that way? *Oh, God. Please. Let them be all right.*

Gradually, the group disbursed to their own cabins or to the bunkhouse, a thick wall of dread hanging over them all.

She didn't know whether to scream or cry or just go to bed, like her father instructed. But there was light coming from the stables. Was that Papa?

A moment later, he emerged from the building on horseback.

She stepped near him. "Where are you going?"

"Why are you still here, Juliana? Go to bed."

"You're going to look for them."

"I know this place blindfolded. I may not find anything, but I'm going to try. The others would only get lost or hurt in the dark."

"I'm going too."

"No."

"Papa! I know this property as well as you do. Don't you remember all those days, those years riding the borders, checking the herd when I was little? This land is as much a part of me as my own skin."

"Juliana—"

"Papa, I have to. I'll be safe—I'll be with *you*. But I won't sleep if you leave me here. Besides, no telling what we'll find. You might need an extra set of hands."

Papa looked at her a long minute. "All right. Tell your mother. I'll saddle Cielito."

Within ten minutes, the two of them headed into the dark, lanterns in hand. They rode without speaking for nearly two hours, along the exact trail the men would have taken. Papa's plan was to cover as much ground as possible, as fast as possible, all the way to the coast. If they found nothing, they'd go slower on the way back.

Several times, she had to remind herself to stay focused on the path. The stars above called to her, like diamonds on velvet, waiting to capture her prayers. Just hours earlier, clouds had covered the sky. Now, not a cloud in sight.

That's when she saw it. "Papa! The rock tower."

Papa looked to the left, on the ridge. There the rock tower, which had been set in place decades ago by Juliana's grandfather, stood like a sentinel, outlined against the sky. Only the top rock, shaped like an arrow, normally pointed to the ocean.

Tonight, it pointed in the opposite direction.

"What in the world?" Papa squinted, as if that might clear his vision and turn the rock around the right way.

Juliana looked from her father back to the tower. Though the top rock was small enough for a single man to turn it, it was high enough he'd need a ladder to reach it. And someone at the bottom to hold him steady. "How could that happen? Who would do such a thing?"

"I don't know. But I doubt it was Miguel or the Ranger. We'll figure it out another time. Let's stay focused on finding them."

Focused. Yes. Juliana needed to focus on locating the lost men...the two men who battled for her heart.

~

Cody gathered enough dry twigs and sticks from under the overhang to start a small fire. Then he'd gone in search of more—that flicker of a blaze wouldn't last long. He finally settled on piles of wind-dried seaweed he'd found wedged under some rocks, adding a little at a time to keep the flame from dying. The stuff put out a lot of smoke, but it was better than nothing. Their clothes were still damp, and the wind off the Gulf made it feel more like December than May.

Beside him, Miguel moaned and shivered.

What time was it? Midnight? Two, three in the morning? His pocket watch had stopped when it was immersed in the sea. "Hang in there, buddy. I'm doing my best."

Having such a small fire might be a blessing in disguise. The shooter was still out there somewhere. A large flame would make them even more of a target, though whoever was out there probably knew exactly where to find them, with or without the light.

Why did they shoot? What had Cody and Miguel stumbled upon, without knowing it? At least Cody now had something worth investigating.

He scratched his head, forced his sleepy eyes open. Surely he'd missed a clue somewhere. All the way here, he hadn't noticed anything strange. No broken branches or recently disturbed earth.

He was too tired to think straight. His guitar was back in his room, as it would have been in the way today. Having some music right about now sure would be nice, though. Softly, he hummed one of the most comforting tunes he knew.

> *Rock of ages, cleft for me*
> *Let me hide myself in Thee . . .*

They were hidden in a rock formation. That brought another hymn to mind:

> *He hideth my soul in the cleft of the rock*
> *That shadows a dry, thirsty land.*

Well, they weren't exactly dry. The water from the canteen was nearly gone, and the hardtack and jerky would only last through morning.

Cody leaned his head against the cold stone wall and closed his eyes, just for a moment. The sounds of his voice blending with Juliana's, just a few nights ago, played through his mind. Would that scene—along with their kiss—torture him the rest of his days?

He grinned. Probably. But oh, what sweet torture.

Miguel muttered something incoherent. Soon, he thrashed his arms, as though fighting invisible demons.

Cody reached a hand to the man's forehead. "Whoa, there. You all right?" Good gravy. The man burned with fever.

Someone would find them early tomorrow. They had to. If not, he might have to hike back and find help.

At least the fire provided some light. Gently, he inspected Miguel's ankle. The other man winced at his touch. He couldn't see the flesh color. But in spite of the cool breeze, the skin around the wound felt like a furnace. Just what he'd feared.

He took the handkerchief that now lay beside Miguel and walked to the water's edge. Bent to soak the cloth with the salt water, to use as a poultice. Behind him, he heard a twig snap.

With lightning-quick reflex, he grabbed the pistol from his holster, cocked it, held it, ready to fire. An energy suffocated the silence, waves crashing in syncopation with his heart.

Someone was out there. He sensed them, though he saw nothing. Slowly, he lowered himself as much as possible and crept to a low-lying scrub oak to use as cover. From here, he could see the dim fire, could see Miguel's still form. At least he wasn't thrashing around. Somehow, Cody had to lead the intruder toward himself, toward the ocean. Miguel was in no way capable of defending himself at the moment.

"I know you're out there!"

Nothing. In his early days as a lawman, he would have chided himself for his overactive imagination. But he'd learned to trust his gut, and his gut said someone was there. Watching. Someone whose intentions weren't good. Man or beast, he wasn't sure. Only that he needed to keep his guard up.

"Show yourself!"

"Ranger! Is that you?" A voice called from the trail—the opposite direction from where he'd heard the stick. Cody swung the gun barrel around but kept himself from pulling the trigger.

In the moonlight, two horse-and-rider outlines appeared from the brush, a halo of light surrounding them. If they carried lanterns, they probably weren't a threat. Ever so slowly, he lowered his aim.

One rider formed a familiar, feminine silhouette. Slowly, carefully, he un-cocked his gun and replaced it at his hip.

"Ranger?" Duke's voice called again from the shadows. A sweeter sound, Cody had never heard.

"Yes, sir." He looked over his shoulder, toward the presence he'd felt just moments earlier. Whoever it was, they were gone. He stepped into the open.

"Miguel with you?"

"Yes, sir. He's injured. To your right. Here, follow me."

"Miguel!" The moment Juliana spotted the man, she climbed from Cielito and ran to kneel beside him. "Oh, Miguel. Look at you!" She opened a satchel and pulled out ministrations, fussing and fretting over his injury.

The distress in her voice stung Cody's heart like the salt water had stung his eyes. "Mr. Duke, may I speak with you in private for a moment?"

"Certainly. What happened?"

Cody filled the man in on the day's events, including the mysterious presence he sensed just before their arrival.

"They shot at you, eh?" Duke's weathered skin stretched tight across his forehead. He looked around the area. "Let's get out of here. Keep your gun at the ready. I'll do the same."

Juliana stroked Miguel's hair away from his forehead. "It will be okay. We'll have you home soon."

Cody gathered Miguel's boots, as well as his own pack, and dropped his hat on his head. "Why don't I ride with Miguel, and the two of you can share a mount."

"No." Duke measured Cody with his eyes. "You've had a hard day, too, son. Miguel can ride with me. You ride with Juliana."

Cody felt Juliana's eyes on him, but when he turned toward her, she looked away. Busied herself with the things she'd removed from that little case of hers, with medicine or whatever she'd used to care for Miguel. Then she climbed onto Cielito and sat, stiff-backed, waiting for him to climb up behind her.

Is this your idea of a test, God? Or some kind of joke, at my expense?

Without speaking, Cody mounted the horse, keeping as

much space between himself and Juliana as possible. He reached around her, trying not to touch her, to grab the reins. All this time, and he still clutched the handkerchief in his hand.

"You don't need to drive. It's my horse. I can steer."

"Uh...sorry. I'm not used to being the passenger. I...don't really know where to put my hands." If he didn't hold the reins, he'd have to grab onto her waist. Or try to sit without holding on to anything, but he'd likely fall backward as the horse moved over this uneven ground.

She sighed. "Fine. Take the reins."

Duke led the way, and Cody steered Cielito behind.

"Interesting choice of a bandana," Juliana said. "What, do you have a girl in every port?"

He couldn't miss the sarcastic tone. "What do you mean?"

"Nothing. I shouldn't have said anything."

"Are you talking about the handkerchief? Don't you recognize it? You made it."

She whipped her neck to the side, to try and look at him. "What are you talking about?"

"This is Miguel's handkerchief. He said you gave it to him."

"I did no such thing. I've never seen that before in my life."

"Really?"

She didn't answer.

Why would she deny giving a token of affection to the man she was about to marry? "Well, he did say that shortly after he swigged a half bottle of whiskey for his leg pain. Maybe he wasn't thinking straight."

"Maybe."

They rode without speaking for a long while. Or at least, they didn't speak with words. But the magnetic pulse between them—the same one from last night—killed him with every bend and sway in the trail, every beat of his heart.

"...and there is a friend that sticketh closer than a brother."
Proverbs 18:24

Juliana felt like every single emotion she'd ever experienced had gotten caught in today's storm, been tossed about, charred by lightning, and left on the beach to fry. Her fear. Her relief at finding them alive. Her heartache over Miguel's leg break—would it ever heal properly? Would he always walk with a limp?

And now.

Now, she hated herself so much for the pleasure she took, resting in Cody's embrace. They rode through the night, step by step, each bounce sending another jolt of electricity through every fiber, every part of her. For several miles, she closed her eyes and tried to pretend it was Miguel's arms surrounding her. But that was no use. As much as she wanted it, Miguel's presence didn't produce this kind of allure.

She thought of Mama and Papa. When she was younger, their obvious attraction for each other embarrassed her. But now, she admired it. Envied it, even. She knew all about their love story—they talked about it to anyone who would listen—and they'd had that kind of spark and sizzle from the beginning. It had grown into a mutual respect, but the sizzle was still there, after all these years.

She didn't feel that way about Miguel. She felt that way about Cody.

What if she told Mama and Papa? And Miguel? What if she followed her heart?

Even then, there was no guarantee this attraction she felt for Cody would be returned. He'd made it clear he didn't want to marry. That he didn't think Rangers and marriage were a good blend.

Behind her, Cody hummed in her ear. *What a Friend We Have in Jesus*...their duet. She felt his humming vibrations through her back, and it felt so sweet, so intimate, she wanted to cry. For right now, for just this moment, she let herself get carried away in the emotion she knew could never last, and added her alto to his tenor.

How could a moment feel so holy and reverent, and yet so passionate at the same time? But it did. It was perhaps the most intimate she'd ever felt with another human being.

They finished the chorus together, and the last strains of their acapella whispers floated away in the wind. Cody breathed deeply, exhaled long and slow, and his breath brushed hot on her hair. Did he feel it too? This pull between them? He must.

But was it as special to him as it was to her? Or was she just another woman in a long list of women? In his line of work, with all his travels, he was bound to meet women who found him attractive.

Now it was her turn to sigh. With Cody Steves, she was barking up an empty tree. Wasn't she?

"Designed any new dresses lately?"

His attempt at conversation made her smile. Here she was, thinking of white-hot passionate love, and he was trying to make small talk. All right, then. "As a matter of fact, I cut out two dresses yesterday for Luisa and Isabel, two of Miguel's nieces. Their mother, Miguel's sister, works in our kitchen."

"Lucky little girls."

They rode a few minutes in silence.

"That night at dinner, you mentioned wanting to design dresses for the masses. Tell me more about that."

"It's just a dream. It's silly, really."

"Why is it silly? You clearly have a gift. I assume you design and sew all your own clothes. I've never seen anything like the dresses you wear. They're all beautiful, and all unique."

"Thank you." The compliment filled a place in her spirit she didn't know was hungry. "I suppose everyone needs an outlet of some kind. But I know my job. My duty."

"And what is that?"

He really wanted to have this conversation? All right. "My duty is to marry Miguel and produce an heir for the Duke Ranch."

He laughed, a low, slow laugh. She wished she could see his face.

"Why is that funny?"

"I suppose it's not funny. It's more tragic, really."

"It's not tragic. Miguel loves me." Yet something in her heart questioned that.

"You're a woman of honor. That's a good thing. Many noble people have married for duty rather than love. But Juliana. You may be a Duke, but your father's ranch isn't a monarchy. You can do what you want, marry who you want. Who's to say your son or daughter won't still take over your father's ranch some-day, even if you don't marry a rancher?"

"I...suppose that's true."

"Even if you never marry. What does the Bible say? What does it profit a man to gain the whole world, if he loses his soul? Something like that."

"Cody, my future is set. It was predetermined before you showed up here, and it will continue to play out after you leave us. I don't know what you're trying to accomplish with this conversation."

"I'm sorry. I didn't mean to upset you. Just trying to pass the miles, I suppose. But Juliana, you're more than a concubine."

"What?" Did he really just say that?

"Please don't take offense. It's just, you're...special. I hate to see you throw away your hopes, your dreams, your talent, just because you don't think you have any other choice."

"What about you, *Ranger* Steves?"

"What do you mean?"

"It's easy for you to comment on my choices, on my future. What about your future? You flirt, then you pull away. You act like because you're a Ranger, you're not allowed to have love. Marriage. Family. Yet I can see you have a tender heart. Surely you want those things. You tell me not to choose duty over love, but that's exactly what you've chosen."

He didn't respond for a good mile or more. Was he angry? Let him be. He had no right to pry into her life, her choices. Especially when he would soon ride away from the Duke Ranch and never look back.

~

*W*ell, that conversation had turned southward pretty quickly. All he'd wanted to do was pass the time and distract himself from her delicious lavender scent, the soft silky caress of her hair on his cheek, and a thousand other sensations he couldn't name. *Ask her about her dresses,* he'd thought. That was a harmless topic.

Harmless, his boot.

How had she managed to turn his simple encouragement around on him? Make it look like he had some kind of ulterior motive, other than to just get through this blasted night? Why did Duke insist Cody and Juliana ride together, anyway? Was the man *trying* to drive Cody mad?

Heavens and mercy.

Thankfully, Duke drew his horse around, waited for them to catch up. "Let's take a quick break. My bones are a little sore."

"Would you like to switch mounts, sir? Ride with your daughter, and let me handle Miguel?"

Miguel let out a snore that could crash timber. He was oblivious to the journey.

"That's all right, son. He's pretty heavy, and I haven't had the day you've had. If you'll just make sure he doesn't fall off while I take care of some personal business, I'll be good."

"Yes, sir." At least he tried. After three hours in the saddle, it did feel good to stretch his muscles. He helped Juliana down, and she disappeared into the brush, the opposite direction from her father. Cody rested one hand on Miguel's back, but every inch of him was on alert. Somewhere out there, a shooter lurked.

Soon, they'd each seen to their needs, taken a bit of water, and eaten a few bites of hard tack. They were as refreshed as they could be in the span of a few minutes. Time to move forward.

"Look. Up ahead. See that rock tower, against the sky?" Juliana's anger seemed to have diminished.

"I do."

"My grandfather built that with Sheriff Gardner's father when they were boys."

"Really? That's interesting."

"You know what's really interesting?"

"I have a feeling you're about to tell me." He thought that would elicit at least a chuckle. Instead, she seemed to tense up.

"The rock on top? The triangular one, that looks like the point of an arrow? It's facing the wrong way."

"What do you mean, the wrong way?"

"It's supposed to point to the ocean. The brush is so thick here, and when Grandpa and Rex Gardner were boys, they'd get to that point and forget which path to take to the beach. They built that tower to point them in the right direction."

"That was smart."

"Yes, it was. It's served as a marker, all these years. But earlier tonight, when Papa and I rode through, we noticed it's facing the wrong way."

Cody looked at the formation. The top rock pointed to his left. "I'm pretty sure that direction still leads to the ocean. It's just a longer path."

"You're right. But Grandpa and Rex had a special place at the beach—where you were. Why would someone change the formation?"

"I don't know. But it bears investigating."

Mr. Duke, who was only a few paces ahead, called over his shoulder. "Ranger, I can't hear everything you're saying, but I assume Juliana's telling you about the rock tower. After we get a few hours of sleep and a hot meal in our bellies, I'd like you and me to come back for a closer look."

"Yes, sir."

Shooting. Changing a decades-old formation. There was definitely something going on in this neck of the Duke property. Finally, something to take his mind off the beautiful girl sharing his saddle.

"Cody?"

"Yeah?"

"I'm sorry I was short with you earlier. I know you were just trying to help. But don't try to give me hope for a different future, all right? I know what's expected of me. And I'm all right with it."

Something about the timbre of her voice, in that moment, reminded him of a broke stallion. Resigned. Submitted. But she was too beautiful to be broken. And the thought of it ripped at his heart.

If he could have a woman like Juliana, he might consider...what? Marriage? Family?

That would be unfair to her. At any time, he could ride away on a horse and come back in a casket. But was that any more unfair than forcing her to marry a man she didn't love, to give up her dreams, all for the mighty dollar? So what if there was no *heir* to the Duke dynasty? It was a great dynasty, for sure. But was it worth more than Juliana's happiness?

Her question earlier came back to him. Why did he think he had to give up his dreams for love and family out of commitment to duty, when he encouraged her to shun duty in favor of her dreams?

Could he have it all? Should he?

That question was one he pondered the rest of the ride back to the Duke Ranch. For one thing he knew: no one had ever made him question his decision, until Miss Juliana Duke rode into his life.

An hour later, they rode their horses into the stable just as the sun yawned and stretched over the horizon. A few men stood in the veranda with coffee mugs in hand. When they saw Mr. Duke, and Miguel leaning against him, they set the mugs aside and scrambled to help.

Duke barked orders to send for the doctor. Within moments, women flooded the area, Miguel's mother and sister and aunts, all clucking and fussing. He looked around, dazed, like he had no idea how he got there.

Cody dismounted, then assisted Juliana from the saddle. "Thank you for sharing your horse with me."

She looked at Miguel, then back at Cody. "Thank you for being my friend." Her tone was wistful. Or maybe just weary.

He watched her walk toward the house, head down, shoulders stooped. Juliana Duke needed to be rescued. Question was, did she *want* to be rescued?

And if so, was he up for the task?

⁓

Juliana vaguely remembered standing by, watching José direct the others to carry Miguel to their cabin so he could tend to the wound. Should she follow? Offer to help? All she wanted was a piece of toast, a hot bath, and her bed.

She stopped by the empty kitchen, grabbed a warm tortilla from its container on the stove, and contemplated which staircase to use. The kitchen stairs were quicker. They were also steeper, and she was bone tired.

"There you are, my love." Mama's voice caressed her like a balm. "Come with me. You can tell me all about your night while I draw you a bath."

She followed her mother to the front staircase and tried to form her thoughts into words. Tried to separate the thoughts she wanted to share with those she wanted to keep to herself. "So much to tell, Mama. Miguel slipped on a rock. That's how his leg was broken. Before that, somebody shot at them. That's when their horses ran away."

Mama set off a fast string of Spanish words of frustration and surprise. When she was upset, she spoke Spanish. When she was calm or wanted to appear in control, she spoke English. After several moments she took a deep breath, turned back Juliana's covers, and said, "What else?"

"I thought you were going to draw me a bath?"

"Ah, yes. The bath." Mama opened the door to the adjoining room with the claw-foot tub. Several years ago, Papa had paid to install indoor pipes to pump hot and cold water throughout the house. Juliana had her own bathing room, as did her parents. The kitchen also had the luxury of hot and cold water on command.

Juliana watched her mother open various jars of oils and powders and drop in a concoction of soothing lavender and mint. Then she helped Juliana out of her riding clothes and into the tub.

Juliana leaned her head against the cool porcelain and closed her eyes. "Thank you."

Mama pulled up a stool next to the tub. "I told you last night everything would be fine, and it will be. You're home, and so is Miguel. It was very brave of you to go after the man you love."

"Mmm-hmmm." Exhaustion and bubbles washed over her.

"Love makes us bold, mija. It makes us do things we wouldn't normally do. I was starting to wonder about your feelings for Miguel, wonder if I'd pushed you into something you weren't ready for. But after last night, I know your love for him is strong. That's how I knew I truly loved your father—when I knew I was willing to die for him. When I knew I'd do anything for him."

The words made Juliana's head ache. Against her will, tears spilled onto her cheeks and plopped into the water.

"Oh, mija! I didn't mean to make you cry. Poor thing. It's been an emotional journey for you. Here. Let's get you dried off and into bed. You'll feel better after you get some sleep."

Juliana didn't protest. Just let her mother dry her off and dress her, like she did when she was four years old. Soon, she snuggled into her soft mattress, and Mama pulled the covers up to her chin. "Sleep, my love. All is well."

But all wasn't well. How could she tell her mother that last night changed nothing about her feelings for Miguel? She hadn't gone after Miguel.

She went after Cody.

And last night was anything but stressful. It was the sweetest, most beautiful night of all her life, riding under the stars with the man whose voice made her heart miss a rhythm, whose touch made her feel like she could fly.

How could she tell Mama that? How could she tell anyone?

She couldn't. Not if she loved them. Because she knew, as much as she knew anything, they depended on her to keep the legacy of Duke Ranch alive. And in order to do that, she needed to marry a rancher.

Not a lawman.

Cody's words to her last night may make sense in his world. But they didn't in hers. Hope? She had no hope. At least not of living her dream. Of owning a dress shop. Of marrying for love.

Her only hope, at this point, was that Cody Steves would ride out of her life soon, and never come back. That he would become a distant, fleeting memory. And that she could somehow content herself with becoming exactly who everybody expected her to be.

CHAPTER 13

"The LORD is my rock, and my fortress, and my deliverer; my God,
my strength, in whom I will trust..."
Psalm 18:2

At two that afternoon, Cody enjoyed a hot breakfast of eggs, sausage, and pancakes, washed down by steaming hot coffee. To say he'd slept like a rock was an understatement. He'd slept like a granite boulder.

"You feel up to riding to the rock tower?" Duke spoke in a low tone. They were the only two in the kitchen—who was he afraid would overhear?

"Sure thing. I'd like to examine it in daylight."

"All right. Have your horse saddled and ready in half an hour."

"I'm coming, too."

Both men turned to Juliana, standing in the doorway, looking astonishingly alluring in men's dungarees and a cowboy hat.

"I thought you were sleeping," Duke told her. "This is men's work. You need to stay here."

"Papa. How could anything possibly happen to me with you and Lt. Steves along? That rock tower is a part of this place, a part of my heritage. Somebody has altered it, and I'm angry. I want to investigate."

"Juliana. I said no."

Cody refrained from comment. On the one hand, he didn't see what harm it could do the investigation for her to tag along. On the other, whenever she was around, his brain didn't seem to work at full capacity.

"If you don't let me come, I'll just investigate on my own when you're not around."

Father and daughter stood there, nose to nose. It seemed odd she would have so much sass about something like this, but tucked her tail and shut her mouth when it came to marrying a man she didn't love. That woman was a puzzle, and he wasn't sure it was in his best interest to keep trying to solve it.

"You are as stubborn as that woman I married. Fine. We leave in twenty-eight minutes."

"Thank you, Papa." She jumped up and down like a twelve-year-old, then kissed her father on the cheek. "I'll meet you at the stables."

"Juliana." Duke called after her. She turned, and Duke leveled a look at Cody, then at his daughter. "Let's try to keep this little excursion between the three of us."

Juliana and Cody both nodded. A moment later, Cody found himself alone in the kitchen again. He walked his dishes to the wash pan and dropped them to soak in the sudsy water. Normally, he would have washed them and put them away himself, but he needed to pack his gear. Mr. Duke was not a man he wanted to cross unless he had to.

In his room, he gathered everything he might need for several days. After yesterday's events, he ought to be more prepared for whatever may come up. Men's voices drifted up through the open window. Duke and...was that the sheriff?

He walked to the window, staying just out of sight. Sheriff Gardner stood on this side of the veranda, discussing something with Duke. He had his horse on a lead, which meant he must have just arrived. The horse whinnied and moved from side to side, demanding attention and a cozy stall.

Duke and Gardner finished their conversation, and Gardner led his horse to the stable. That's when Cody noticed the hoof-print. Was that the same mark he'd seen on the beach? He squinted, trying to make it out. He needed a closer look.

He left his pack open on his bed and raced down the stairs. He slowed his walk before he exited the house. No need to draw attention. As casually as possible, he ambled over to the spot where the two men had stood and knelt to examine the prints.

Crack on the upper right curve, with a little curl at the bottom.

It was the same mark.

In his line of work, Cody was rarely surprised by anything. And honestly, he'd felt something was off with the man from the day he met him. But to shoot at them? Try to kill them? Why in the world would a man of the law do such a thing?

Only one answer made sense. Gardner must be working with the rustlers. The thought sickened Cody. Now he had to figure out how to convince Duke. How to arrest the man, and all those working with him. For now, he needed to play dumb. If Gardner suspected he knew anything, Cody might end up on the wrong side of a bullet.

He went back to his room, gathered his things, and made his way to the stables. Gardner was gone, his horse already settled. Cody looked around. He was still a few minutes early. No one in sight.

"Hey, girl." Cody nuzzled the horse. Across the room, Atlas nickered. *Jealous.* Cody ignored Atlas and kept talking, low and slow, to the horse in front of him. "You're a pretty girl. Can I get a look at that foot? Let me see..."

He moved inside the stall, rubbing the horse with gentle strokes. Slowly, calmly, he lifted the horse's right hoof. Knelt on one knee. Looked at the shoe.

Yep. Same horse.

"Can I help you, Ranger?" Sheriff Gardner glared at him from the stable door.

"Just admiring your horse. She's a beauty."

Gardner stepped in front of the stall, blocking Cody's exit. "Yes, she is."

"I...always admire fine horse stock. What is she? Part Palomino?"

"That's right. A better horse, you'll never find."

"Oh, Atlas is a pretty good steed. But he's a lot bigger. Not nearly as fast, I'm sure."

"Probably not." Gardner kept his gaze locked on Cody but stepped aside. "I'm sorry to hear about the trouble you and Miguel had last night. Sounds like you stumbled on something out there."

"Seems so." Cody pulled Atlas's saddle from its place on the wall. Folded his blanket over his body. Continued readying him for their journey.

"I guess we need to send some more men that way to investigate closer."

"Probably a good idea." *This whole thing was a setup.*

"Where you headed now?"

Let's try to keep this little excursion between the three of us. "Since I was separated from Atlas all night, I want to ride him, make sure he's okay."

"Sounds like a good idea. I'll see you later." Gardner walked away with one final look over his shoulder.

Cody led Atlas into the sunshine just as Duke approached. "I'll meet you and Juliana at the pass. I want to take Atlas on a little detour first."

Duke looked at Gardner's retreating figure and nodded. "I understand."

Cody caught just a glimpse of Juliana as he and Atlas loped toward the canyon. He'd go partway, circle around and cut back. This would give him time to figure out how to break the news to Duke.

~

Juliana clutched the basket of sopapillas Mama had put together, along with a jar of honey, for her to take to Miguel. "With a man, food fixes almost anything, mija. Food and a pretty face, anyway. Take this to him, and he'll be feeling better in no time. But, oh, my goodness. Get out of those awful men's clothes before you go!"

"I'm going riding with Papa. And I don't think Miguel will care. He's seen me in worse."

Mama smiled. "You're probably right. Oh, you and Miguel will make such pretty babies."

"Mama!" Heat scorched Juliana's cheeks.

"I'm sorry, mija. But it's true."

The thought of doing...*that*...with Miguel brought a wave of nausea. She didn't know why. He was perfectly handsome. Apparently, *all the girls* thought so. Juliana thought back to Luisa's statement yesterday. It was nothing, of course. It meant nothing. Just two little girls being silly. They probably thought their uncle was handsome, so they assumed everyone else did, too. Which, he was.

Juliana had about ten minutes before she needed to meet her father and Cody. Ten minutes to visit Miguel in his sickbed and convince her cheating heart that *he* was her man. Not Cody. *Please, God. Help me love him. I know he's the one I'm supposed to love. I don't know what's wrong with me...but I need Your help.*

She turned the corner to his family's cabin and saw a flash of white skirt, a flash of light brown hair turning the other corner. Who was that? She didn't recognize them as one of the workers' daughters. Why, it almost liked like...

No, that was silly. What would Emily be doing out here, at this time of day? It was probably Teresa, or Caroline, or one of Miguel's numerous aunts or cousins. Many of his relatives lived just across the border. Sometimes they came for a visit and left, and the Dukes didn't know about it until later. They probably heard about Miguel's leg.

She tapped gently. He might be sleeping, and she didn't want to waken him.

"Come in."

She pushed open the heavy wooden door. Miguel was on the sofa, his leg propped on some pillows. "I brought you something."

"There's my beautiful girl. All you need to bring is your smile, and my day is full of sunshine."

She blushed. More from shame than pleasure.

"Come. Sit by me."

"I can't stay. But I thought you might like these. They're from Mama, actually. I slept until an hour ago."

Miguel chuckled. "I haven't been awake very long myself. To be honest, I don't remember much about last night. Or yesterday, for that matter."

"The Ranger said you drained the whiskey bottle."

"Yeah. I don't know what came over me."

"Pain, I'm sure. Anyway, I'm sorry about your leg. But I'm glad it's not worse."

A wicked gleam came into Miguel's eye, along with a half-grin she was sure would cause most girls' hearts to flutter. "Come here."

"What? I'm right here."

"No. I mean, lean a little closer."

She leaned in, thinking he wanted to tell her something. He

gently placed his hand on her neck and drew her in for a kiss. *A kiss!* At the last moment, she turned her head, and his lips landed on her cheek.

He chuckled again. "You can't blame a guy for trying."

She smiled. "No. I suppose not."

"I'll try again."

She was an awful person. Awful, awful, awful. "I know." Heat flooded her face, and he smiled, a gentle, teasing smile. *Oh, dear Lord. He thinks I've never kissed a man. I am a wretched, horrible person!*

God, I want to love this man. I need to love this man. Help me love this man.

Without thinking through her next action, she leaned forward and gave him a big, wet, sloppy kiss, then pulled back. The surprise on his face mirrored her own. *That did not go well.*

But his grin told her he thought it went quite well. "Wow. Thank you."

"Uh...you're welcome. I need to go."

"No, wait." His eyes grew serious. "What would you think about moving up our wedding date?"

What? "Why?"

He grinned. "I'm just ready to move on with the happily ever after part of our lives."

"I...don't know."

"Just think about it, all right? I'm laid up here, unable to get around, and I've been thinking. And I've come to the conclusion that long engagements are for the birds. I can't work for a while, but soon I'll be able to limp down the aisle. I've waited a long time for you, Juliana. Don't make me wait any longer."

What could she say to that? "I'll think about it."

He squeezed her hand. She pulled loose with a little wave. Without looking back, she left the cabin and shut the door behind her.

She walked—more of a walk-run—to the stables, where Papa waited with Cielito, already saddled and ready.

"You've been to see Miguel." It was a statement, not a question. He looked pleased.

"Yes."

"How is he? I'm sure better, once he saw you." Warmth flooded her face again, and Papa grinned. "Ah. Young love."

"He seemed fine." She mounted Cielito. "Where's the Ranger?"

"He'll meet us at the pass. Let's go."

~

Cody examined the rock tower and tried to ignore the woman standing just to his left. "It's a solid structure. It would take at least two men and two ladders to get that high, to change the direction of that top rock."

"My father and Rex Gardner were teens when they built it. I remember Dad saying they used a ramp to roll the rocks to the top. They were quite proud of it."

Cody studied the dirt surrounding the tower for the third time. No prints. No ladder marks. Yesterday's storm had wiped out any trace of tracks. He cleared his throat. "Speaking of Gardner... I have something I need to share with you."

"I'm listening." Duke stopped his study of the lower rocks and looked at Cody. Juliana did the same.

"I told you about the unique hoof print in the sand. Today, I discovered whose horse it belonged to."

Duke said nothing, like he waited for more of an explanation.

"It's from the sheriff's horse."

Duke shifted from one foot to the other, looked at the ground, then back at Cody.

"What are you saying?"

"I'm saying it was Gardner who shot at us. Or at least, he had something to do with it."

"Look here, son. I know you're a high-fallutin' Texas Ranger and all. That's why I called you here. But John Gardner and I have been friends our entire lives. He's like a brother to me. If I were you, I'd watch where you're stepping."

Cody held the man's eyes. If fire could have shot from Duke's glare, Cody would be a melted pile of lava right about now. "I saw the tracks. I examined the horse."

"I'm sure there's a logical explanation. Maybe somebody stole his horse."

"He didn't mention—"

"That's enough, son. You're sittin' on an empty nest."

"With all due respect, sir, I—"

"I said, that's all. I'm done with this conversation. Juliana, get ready. We're heading back."

Juliana offered a long, sympathetic look, but she said nothing to contradict her father. For all her bravado in the kitchen earlier today, she sure had turned into a meek little thing. Or maybe, like her father, she was certain of Gardner's innocence. *I'm sorry*, she mouthed, just before she mounted her horse.

Cody nodded, though he really didn't understand these people at all. "If you don't mind, I'm gonna stay here. Look around some more. I may do some exploring of my own."

"Suit yourself." Duke clicked to his horse and left in a spray of mud, Juliana close at his heels.

He stayed another ten minutes, maybe. Just long enough to regain his senses after that baffling exchange. What to do, what to do? What would Rett do, in this situation?

He'd probably talk to Elizabeth and get her input. Those two were a great team.

Cody looked at the arrow rock, at the direction it pointed. It led away from the well-worn trail. He rode up and down the path several times before he saw it. The brush blended in well with the plants around it, but...there. It had been pulled into place. He hopped down, moved things around. Sure enough, there was a narrow trail. Still not big enough for cattle to trample through, but worth investigating, all the same.

He followed it for a couple of miles. If it led all the way to the ocean, it would take a couple more hours or more. There was barely enough room to turn Atlas around, and the horse whickered a complaint at the stinging brush and briars, but eventually they reversed their direction and headed back to the main path. He'd return first thing in the morning so he could have all day to investigate. For now, he'd circle back around the long way. He wanted to get a closer look at the Mustang Caves.

"Some trust in chariots, and some in horses; but we will remember the name of the Lord our God."
Psalm 20:7

Papa said little on the way back to the house. Juliana knew better than to talk to him when he was like this. Mama? Mama could say anything to the man, anytime, and he'd listen. But if Juliana tried to coax him to consider Cody's viewpoint, Papa would just tell her to hush up.

Sheriff Gardner had never been her favorite person. He seemed sullen and judgmental. But Papa had his reasons for loving the man, and she couldn't fault her father for his loyalty. After all, loyalty ran thick in their blood. It was the reason she would marry Miguel.

When they rode into the yard, she didn't follow Papa into the stables. She wasn't ready to stop riding. In the corral, Luisa and Isabel rode two of the older horses around the ring. Carlos, their father, worked nearby, mending a portion of the corral fence.

"Hi Juliana!" The girls waved, grins plastered on their delighted faces.

"Look at you. You're master riders. When did you become so adept in the saddle?"

"Adept?"

"It means you look like you know what you're doing."

"We do. Papa's giving us riding lessons."

Juliana studied the two mares a moment. Tame was an understatement. She pulled Cielito's reins toward Carlos. "Do you think they're ready to go for a short ride with me?"

Carlos removed his hat and squinted up at her. "If it's a short ride. Dinner's in an hour."

"I'll have them back before then. I promise."

The man nodded and went back to the fence.

"Girls. Follow me. Your father said we could go for a real ride."

They squealed, and Juliana laughed. Being their aunt was a definite perk to marrying Miguel. Maybe if she thought about it harder, she'd find more perks. The corral gate squeaked as she pulled the rope to open it, and the girls passed through. "Let's go."

She rode nice and easy into open range so the girls could come alongside her. They chattered about the upcoming wedding and asked if she'd worked on their dresses any more, then changed the subject to Pepito, their pet dog, before she had a chance to answer. Just ahead was the ridge to Mustang Valley. She'd show them the view, then they'd head back.

~

Cody sensed, more than saw, human presence in the caves. He looped Atlas's reins around a tree limb several hundred yards back and crept the rest of the way on foot, low and slow, praying he wasn't detected. Sure enough, as he drew closer, he heard voices.

He pressed himself against the rock and sneaked closer, trying to make out the conversation. It was Gardner's voice. A few others he didn't recognize. And...was that José?

"Move the wedding up. It's the only way." Gardner. Did he mean Juliana's wedding?

"His leg is broken. He can't even walk down the aisle." José.

"Use that as the reason. He can't work now. He might as well get married and have his honeymoon. The sooner we get them married, the sooner we can do away with Oscar and Maria."

Do away with? A cold chill snaked through Cody's veins.

"I know. But if we move too fast, Juliana may back out. If she doesn't marry Miguel, we've got nothing."

Cody wanted to vomit.

"Then tell him to use that pretty-boy charm of his and win her over."

"He's trying. I think he's making progress."

"Good. We need control of this ranch. The sooner the better."

He had to find Juliana. He tried to move back the way he'd come, but a rock broke loose beneath his foot. His boot slid, and the sound echoed through the canyon. Next thing he knew, men shouted behind him. He ran, full speed, to Atlas. A bullet sped past his head, then another. *Oh, God. Get me out of here.*

In one smooth leap, he landed in the saddle, and Atlas sped into the thin oak-and-pine forest. Cody grabbed his pistol from his holster and shot over his shoulder, hoping to at least scare them back. On the other side of this copse was a clearing where he'd be an open target. But if he stayed in this crop of trees, they'd have him surrounded in no time.

He pulled Atlas to a stop behind the largest tree he could find. Bullets banged and whizzed; one landed in a limb not four feet from him. Up ahead was another rocky hill. If he could get behind it, he might have a chance. From there, he could make it over the ridge and back to the house to tell Mr. Duke. Would Duke even believe him?

Hugging his body low against Atlas, he whispered, "Okay, boy. I know you're big, and speed isn't your strong point. But you're smart. That's why I chose you over every other horse I could have. Right now, though, I need you to run like the wind. Can you do that, boy? I know you can. Come on. Hyah!"

Atlas might as well have grown wings in that moment. The horse bolted from the thicket, up the hill, and to the other side. Somehow, through a miracle of God, they made it without getting hit.

⁓

They had just topped the ridge. Juliana lifted her arm to point to the place she most often saw mustangs, when shots rang out. The girls screamed. Everything seemed to speed up and slow down at the same time. She had to get the girls to safety, now! But how?

Where did the shots come from?

The caves.

They needed to turn around.

"Girls! Look at me." She screamed to get their attention. Their panic-filled eyes met hers. "Lean down as low as you can on your horses, like this. Stay close to the tree line. We'll ride back to the house as fast as we can. Whatever you do, don't stop. All right?"

The girls nodded, and Juliana took off, looking over her shoulder to make sure they followed. Hoofbeats competed with gunfire, sweat with gunpowder. She held Cielito back, since he was faster than the girls' horses. She glanced behind every few beats to make sure children and horses were close. "Keep up!"

A high-pitched sound pierced the din. A scream! She pulled

Cielito to a stop, but motioned for Isabel to keep going. Luisa's horse followed. Where was Luisa?

Juliana's lungs tightened.

She couldn't get air.

Don't panic.

She jumped off Cielito. Retraced her steps, staying in the shadows. "Luisa!"

There she was. Within the tree line. She wasn't moving.

Oh, God. Please. Help!

~

Cody sensed riders closing in on him, but he kept riding, kept shooting behind, kept praying. Prayer and gunshot—that was all he had at this point. The ridge was just ahead, if he could make it—

Juliana! Riding just ahead with two little girls! Surely the men behind would see and cease fire. Yet the shots continued.

As quick as they appeared, the three females disappeared behind the ridge. Cody topped the high point and pulled Atlas into the open, away from the direction the girls went. At least he could direct the gunfire away from them. He caught a glimpse of the three riders just as they sped around a curve ahead. Good.

But wait—one little girl flew off her horse. Had she been hit, or just fallen?

He couldn't tell. He had to check on her.

They'd catch him for sure. Maybe kill him.

But if they didn't see her fall, they might trample her.

Cody jumped from Atlas before he'd come to a full stop and ran to the small, prone figure. Something thudded into his left shoulder. Pain like a hot poker seared his left arm, tangled through his chest.

He kept going.

Had to…get the…girl.

Through gritted teeth, he knelt over her. Forced the fog in his head to the side.

Focus. It didn't look like she'd been shot. Her head had a bad gash.

Men behind him shouted. The shooting paused.

Cody's vision blurred.

On the ridge, several men lined up. He couldn't make out their faces. But they saw him. They had to see the girl, now in his arms.

He bit back the screaming, searing pain. Picked her up, set her in the saddle.

Looked at them so they knew that he saw them too.

Used every bit of remaining strength to climb back on Atlas.

If they shot him, they shot him. With his back to the men who wanted him dead, he cradled his young cargo and rode slow and steady back toward the house.

Juliana waited up ahead, alone, her face drained of color. "Is Luisa all right? Was she shot? Oh! You're hurt."

"I think she…just fell. Hit her…head on…a rock."

"Here. Let me take her. Can you make it back?"

"Leave her where she is. I'm all right." It was a lie. But with Luisa in his arms, he had more reason to stay coherent.

"Who were those men? Why were they shooting? Cody, what's happening? Are those the rustlers?"

For the second time today, Cody felt he'd lose his breakfast. "Maybe."

"They're still back there."

Cody swallowed. "They won't follow us."

Juliana studied the girl in his arms. She had a sizable goose egg, already turning purple. At least there was no indentation— a good sign. Her steady breathing, also a good sign.

She studied Cody's shoulder. Lifted up her skirt and tore a

long strip from her petticoat. "Hold still." She wrapped the strip as many times as she could around the wound. "Maybe that'll help until we get you home. Can you make it?"

Cody nodded. "Let's go." Cody had no desire to hang around. He'd lost a lot of blood already. He could feel it.

Thankfully, they didn't talk on the ride back.

What was there to say? Could he even form…words, if he wanted to?

Thoughts flooded his conscious, his subconscious. How would he…convince Duke that Gardner wanted…to kill him? And Miguel…was in on it.

Maybe being rich…wasn't as great as it seemed. You could never…be sure…who your friends were.

Luisa moaned. Her eyes fluttered open, and she looked at Cody, confusion clouding her eyes.

"Hey there. You had quite a fall." He pushed to make his voice sound normal.

"Did they shoot me?"

"No."

"Did they shoot you?"

"Yeah."

"My head hurts."

"It'll probably…hurt for a few days."

Mr. Duke waited for them, gun in hand. His wife stood behind him. When she saw Luisa, she stepped forward and took the child.

"What in the world was all that ruckus?"

"Papa, he's hurt. He needs a doctor."

"I'm…fine. Can we go…someplace…pri…vate, sir? I have a lot to…

Everything went black.

~

"Cody!" Juliana's heart pounded in her ears. She slid out of her saddle in time to keep Cody from falling off his horse, but he was heavy, and she didn't know how long she could hold him there.

"I've got him." From Atlas's opposite side, Papa reached his big arms around Cody. "Get a chair—or drag one of those tables over here. I need something to pull him onto."

Juliana released her hold on Cody and found the nearest table. Solid wood—but she was too small to move it. She grabbed a chair and pulled it close, then helped Papa maneuver Cody into it.

"Dr. Gold is here checking on Miguel. Run get him. Quick!"

Of all those times Papa's barking orders frustrated her, this was not one of them. She was glad to be told what to do, to not have to make a decision.

She flew to Miguel's cabin, banged twice, then crashed through the door. "Doctor, come now. It's an emergency." Her eyes briefly met Miguel's, and he smiled like he thought she'd come to see him.

She averted her eyes, looking around the small room, at the chair, at the mantel, anywhere but at him. She couldn't deal with him right now. Couldn't deal with the warring emotions that came with his presence. Not when Cody lay dying.

She walked outside to wait on the porch while Dr. Gold said a few words to Miguel and gathered his things. Two doors down, she saw Mama in the doorway to Luisa and Isabel's house. She looked back at the doctor—what was taking him so long?

The man picked up his bag and followed her across the opening, around the house to where Papa stood next to Cody. "What happened?"

"We don't know exactly. I heard gunshots." Papa moved aside to the give the doctor room.

"I saw what happened. Men chased Cody out of Mustang Canyon. I didn't see who. The girls and I tried to get away, but Luisa fell off her horse. Cody risked his life to get her out of harm's way."

"What were you doing out there with the girls?"

"I took them on a ride. I—it doesn't matter. Doctor, will he be all right?"

"I'll need to do surgery, to remove the bullet. Duke, get some of your men to help me move him."

"Where is everyone?" Papa growled. "Isaac! Cade!"

Cade appeared from the corral. "Yes, sir? Oh, man!"

Soon, Isaac came from the foundry. Together, they part-carried, part-dragged the chair—with Cody in it—into the empty kitchen, gently lifted him on the big butcher-block table, and stepped aside.

"What's going on here?" Sheriff Gardner charged in like a knight on a mission. "Is everyone all right?"

"Not everyone." Papa nodded to the table, where Cody lay.

He looked white, pasty. That beautiful, golden tan was gone, replaced with a sickly-gray pallor. Would he live? *Please God. Let him live.*

"I'll need an assistant." Dr. Gold spoke to whoever would listen. The men in the room, looked at each other, as if waiting for someone else to volunteer.

"I'll do it." Juliana stepped forward.

"Juliana, you can't—"

"I can, Papa. And I will." Her tone came out stronger than she felt. She had to do *something.* If Cody died because he saved Luisa, wouldn't that really be her fault? For taking the girls for a ride? She couldn't sort through the logic right now. She only knew Cody needed her, and she would stay right here until she knew he would be all right. *He had to be all right.*

An hour later, Juliana's dress was covered in blood. *Cody's blood.* A bullet clinked into the white porcelain bowl she'd set out for that specific purpose. Could they trace the bullet to a specific gun? She listened for Dr. Gold's soft orders: Laudanum. Alcohol. Gauze. Needle, thread.

Her thoughts were absorbed with Cody's chest, with the ragged up-down, up-down motion. A couple times it went down and failed to rise again for too long. Then her own breathing would fail, for many seconds, until he took another breath, like her ability to keep breathing was tied to his.

After a long time, Dr. Gold placed his instruments on a cloth, walked to the sink, and washed his hands. "We've done all we can."

"Will he...?"

"I don't know. He lost a lot of blood. If we can get him through the next twenty-four hours, he should be all right. This next day will determine a lot."

"What can I do?"

"Stay close. Watch his breathing and watch for a fever. If his temperature spikes, cool his head with a wet cloth. If he stops breathing, talk to him. Make some noise. It will remind him he's alive, give him a reason to fight." He took the cloth with his soiled instruments to the sink and ran water over them.

At that moment, Papa entered the kitchen, Sheriff Gardner behind him. "How's he doing, Doc?"

Juliana lifted Cody's hand, entwined his fingers with hers. The men's voices buzzed behind her like a mosquito in the room. *Cody.* Golden hairs peeked above the carefully wrapped bandages on his chest. Up...down. Up...down. Up...*Come on, Cody.* Down.

She heard her name, like an echo at the far end of a tunnel, but didn't respond.

"Juliana." Papa's hand rested on her shoulder. "Come. You've done enough."

"No. I have to make sure he's all right."

"We'll take care of him the best we can. It's not your place."

How could she tell him? It *was* her place. Oh, how she didn't want it to be. How she wanted to be who they wanted her to be, love who they wanted her to love. But her heart had betrayed her in the worst possible way. It had gotten away from her and landed on this man who lay dying on the table.

"Come on." He pulled her, gently, firmly, toward the hall. "Dr. Gold will stay with him until we locate someone to keep watch. Get cleaned up."

Tears blurred her vision, clotted her words. "Papa, I—I need to stay with him."

Papa looked at her, understanding straining his features. "Juliana. No."

"Yes. I—"

"No. Juliana, Cody isn't who you think he is. Isn't who any of us thought he was. I didn't want to tell you this, but Cody Steves fired the first shot out there. He fired at the sheriff, and at José. He's a loose cannon, Juliana. As soon as he's well enough to travel, he's leaving here."

"What? That can't be right."

Sheriff Gardner stepped from the shadows. "I'm afraid it's the truth. These Rangers, they're a hard bunch. They shoot first, ask questions later."

That didn't sound like Cody.

"We're lucky no one was killed today. And that little girl...when I think of what could have happened because of Ranger Steves' actions, I...I'm just glad God was on our side."

Juliana looked at the sheriff, held his eyes. The man blinked. Looked away before looking back at her. Something wasn't right. That man was lying.

He had to be.

If he wasn't, that meant...it meant she'd given her heart to the wrong man.

"I…need to go."

Suddenly, there was Mama. "Come with me, mija. Let's get you cleaned up."

CHAPTER 15

"I will cry unto God most high..."
Psalm 57:2

ody heard voices. Faraway voices, and it sounded like he was under water. He tried to open his eyes, but they wouldn't cooperate. What was going on with his chest? It felt like somebody was sitting on it, and he couldn't breathe. After fighting for strength for—he couldn't tell how long—he finally fluttered his eyes open, only to squeeze them shut against the bright light.

"Can you hear me, Ranger?" He didn't know the voice. Cody grunted. His throat was dry, and his tongue felt too big for his mouth.

"I'm Dr. Gold. You were shot in the shoulder. Yesterday, I removed the bullet."

Cody forced his eyes open, forced them to focus in on the man talking. Shot? Bullet removed? It didn't make any sense.

Slow, hazy memories pressed his conscious mind.

Caves.

Shooting.

A little girl.

Juliana. *Juliana! Was she all right?*

He must have said her name out loud, because Dr. Gold said, "Miss Duke is fine. We're all just concerned about you. Although I feel much better now that you're awake. We weren't sure you'd make it."

Cody tried to sit up, but pain like a thousand knives sliced through his shoulder and down his back. He gasped.

"Steady, now. Try to stay still. Take some deep, slow breaths into your gut. That's right. I can give you something for the pain, but first, Mr. Duke would like to talk to you. Do you think you can answer a few questions?"

He forced a nod. He'd do his best. He had to tell Duke what he'd heard.

"Good morning, Lt. Steves." Duke's voice came from his other side. He turned his head that way and tried to focus on the man's hazy form. "I've got Sheriff Gardner here. He tells me you opened fire on him and some other men yesterday. Is that true?"

Opened fire? What had Gardner told him? He swallowed. His lips were dry. He licked them, then croaked out, "No."

Duke held a cup of water to his lips. The cool liquid felt like heaven sliding down his throat. "I know it's hard for you to talk. But when you're able, I need you to tell me your side of the story."

The water rejuvenated him enough to say, "That's a lie."

Somebody laughed, a long, low chuckle. *Gardner.*

Duke turned. "He might talk more if you're not in here, John."

"I'll leave."

Cody heard a door open, then close. Heard a scraping sound, as Duke pulled a chair next to the bed. "I need you to tell me what you remember about yesterday."

"Here, son. Let me help you sit up." Dr. Gold and Duke

helped shift him in the bed and added another pillow or two behind him.

Cody winced at the discomfort but didn't complain. Pain, he could handle. "More water," he croaked.

Duke held the cup to his mouth again. "I know you're uncomfortable. But tell me what you can."

"After..." Cody sucked in a breath. Closed his eyes and tried to gather his thoughts. "After I left you...yesterday, I circled back...to Mustang Caves. Perfect hiding place for...rustlers. When I got close to one of the...caves, I heard voices, so I sneaked in. I heard the sheriff...José, and some others. They have plans...to take over...your ranch."

Cody paused. The energy drained from him, but he had to keep going. Had to tell Duke what he'd heard.

"That's a pretty stiff accusation." Duke's voice held no judgment, but his face was inscrutable.

"When Miguel and...Juliana marry, they...plan to kill...you and your wife."

Duke stood. Walked to the window.

Cody closed his eyes. *God, give me the words. The strength. Let him listen.*

"I knew I had to...tell you their...plan. When I tried to...leave, my boot...slipped on a rock and they...heard me. They came...after me."

Duke returned to the chair. "Juliana said you risked your life to rescue Luisa. That's commendable."

Cody didn't respond. Closed his eyes. Wanted sleep.

Somebody knocked on the door. He opened his eyes for just a moment, just long enough to see Juliana enter. He tried to smile. So...pretty.

"The sheriff said he was awake. I wanted to see for myself."

His lids were...so heavy. A soft, small hand touched his own hand, Juliana's fingers brushing along his skin.

"He'll be all right?" Juliana's voice was barely more than a whisper.

"He'll live." Duke's chair scraped again. His boots thudded on the floor, toward the door. "Right now, there's no point trying to talk to him. He's hallucinating."

~

"Hallucinating?" Juliana looked again at Cody. His eyes fluttered like he wanted to stay awake but couldn't. "What did he say?"

"A bunch of nonsense." Papa shook his head. "I'm starting to question the purpose of calling in the Texas Rangers. This pup's too wet behind the ears to solve a case like this. Apparently, he wants to solve it so bad, he's making things up."

"Papa! I don't think—"

"Juliana, I know you like the Ranger. And I can see why— he's a likable fellow. But being likable doesn't make him competent. As soon as he's able, I'm sending him home."

"Papa! You haven't given him a ch—"

"That's enough, Juliana. Instead of gawping over Lt. Steves, you ought to be seeing to your fiancé. Or have you forgotten you have one of those?"

Juliana bit back the harsh words she wanted to say. If she argued, she'd only make things harder for Cody. She was about to drop his hand and drag herself to Miguel's cabin when the door opened again.

It was Sheriff Gardner. Emily came in behind him. What was she doing here?

"Oscar, I'm sorry to interrupt again, but this is important."

Juliana stood. "I was just leaving."

"No. Juliana, I think you should stay and hear what Emily has to say."

Emily looked at Juliana, her chin high, her jaw set. Why did she despise Juliana so? What happened to the friendship they once shared?

"What is it, Emily?" Papa's tone had that overly polite sound. The sound most people wouldn't question. The sound Juliana knew all too well, that signaled he'd about had enough.

"I...don't mean to cause trouble. Perhaps I should have spoken sooner, but I...I didn't know what to... I mean..."

"Out with it, girl!" Gardner huffed.

Emily looked at her father, then at Juliana, and set her shoulders back. She shifted her gaze to Papa. "On the night of the engagement party for Juliana and Miguel, I saw her kissing Lt. Steves."

All the blood drained from Juliana's body. Through her feet. Into the floorboards.

Papa's eyes swung to her. "Is this true, Juliana?"

She dropped to the chair. "I...uh..."

"I asked a simple question. Yes or no will suffice."

All the blood suddenly reappeared, every bit of it in her cheeks. "Yes." She barely got the word out, but it was enough. Enough for everyone in the room—Sheriff Gardner, Dr. Gold, Emily, Papa—to hear. She stared at her feet. Watched fat teardrops make plop-plop splashes on the floor next to her boots.

For the longest minute in history, there was no other sound in the room. It was as if time stopped in order to fully document her humiliation, to seal her fate as a tramp, a harlot, a fallen woman.

Finally, Papa shifted. "I'll see you in my study in ten minutes, Juliana." He left the room, his footsteps heavy and solid. Gardner followed him. Emily stood there a moment, as if wanting to say more, but Juliana refused to acknowledge the girl. Her former friend. Why would she do such a thing?

After a time, Emily left.

Juliana almost forgot Dr. Gold was in the room until the

older man walked behind her and set a gentle hand on her shoulder. Soft as a morning dove cooing to its young, he said, "I know this seems like a terrible thing to you, Miss Duke. But one day, when you are old like I am, this will be just a tiny little story in the thick, leather-bound volume of your life. It will be all right. I promise."

Juliana nodded, not because she agreed, but because she didn't know what else to do. Things would never be all right again.

"You'd better go. Your father's waiting."

With another nod, Juliana stood. Looked over her shoulder at Cody's sleeping form. Was it worth it? That kiss?

She inhaled a long, shaky breath and a short, shaky prayer. *I don't know what to do, God. Help me.*

The hallway leading to Papa's study stretched into forever. She passed the landing, overlooking the massive marble entry. Emily and the sheriff stood to one side, whispering. They looked up at her as she passed, but she didn't react to them.

Mama was with Papa in the study. When Juliana entered, Mama dragged her into a tight embrace. "Mija. My girl. I didn't know your feelings had gotten so tangled." She led her to the overstuffed sofa, sat beside her, and pulled Juliana's head onto her shoulder.

Papa sat behind his desk, leaned back, and steepled his fingers.

"I'm so sorry..." Juliana gulped back a sob.

"You have nothing to be sorry for. I had no idea that scalawag..." The skin around Papa's mouth was white, his eyes slightly bulging.

"Papa, it's not—"

"You do not need to explain yourself. I trusted that man. In my home! I'm so sorry, baby girl. I should never have put you in that position. Should never have let a man I barely know stay right here in this house. What was I thinking?"

Mama stroked Juliana's hair. "I'll tell you what you were thinking, Oscar. You were thinking the man is a Texas Ranger. A lawman. When you learned he'd saved Juliana's life from that snake, you wanted to repay him. You have a kind, generous heart. This is not your fault. How could we know he was an even bigger snake than the one he shot?"

Juliana pulled away from her mother. "You're wrong. You're both wrong. You don't know him like I—"

"I know he drew you in." Papa's sad eyes held no judgment. At least not for her. "You're innocent. Thank God we found out before something even worse happened."

God. Help them understand. Show me what to say. Despite her inner pleading, nothing came to mind. She had no idea how to explain to her parents that her feelings for Cody were real. That he hadn't set a trap for her. That she...oh, molasses. How could she tell them that *she* kissed *him,* and not the other way around? "Does Miguel know?" She wasn't sure why she asked that. She just wanted to know how to proceed.

"I asked John and Emily to keep it to themselves. You should probably tell him." Papa hung his head.

"Miguel loves you, Juliana." Mama spoke with certainty. "He will be hurt. But his anger will burn toward the Ranger, not you. He will forgive, and you will move on with the wedding."

It all sounded so final. They really couldn't see. How could they know her so well, and know her so little?

Papa stood up, walked around his desk, and sat on its edge. "No more checking on Lt. Steves while he's here. Understand? Stay away from him. I don't want to see you even looking toward his room."

"I agree." Mama folded her hands in her lap. "Go to your room. Wash your face. Then check on Miguel. That is where your heart belongs. That is where you'll be safe and loved."

She might as well have been standing in someone else's

body, living someone else's life. None of it made sense, yet she knew her fate was sealed.

What, did she think she could just ride off into the sunset with Cody Steves? Leave her family with no heir, and never look back?

Of course not.

They were wrong about Cody, but that didn't change her destiny. Without a word, she nodded and left the room. Perhaps this was best. The sooner she didn't have to look at Cody, the sooner she could carry on with her duties as the only child of Oscar and Maria Duke.

As she walked the hallway that led back to her room, she paused in front of the big, oak door that led to the guest wing. *Please, God. Let him be all right.*

And let me forget how I feel about him.

CHAPTER 16

"Let the weak say I am strong..."
Joel 3:10

When Cody awoke, he didn't know where he was. Didn't know the strange man who sat by his bed, though something in his memory said the man was a doctor.

"Welcome back to the land of the living."

Cody tried to sit up, but the pain in his shoulder bit like a scorpion. Like an avalanche, it all came back to him. The caves. The shooting. Luisa. Even...did he talk to Duke, or did he dream that?

"Here. Let me help you." The man moved to his side, but Cody waved him away. "I'm fine. I just need to..." He pushed himself up further on his good elbow. "Where are my boots?"

"I hardly think you need your boots, Lt. Steves."

"I'm sorry. Who are you?"

"I'm Dr. Gold. Normally, I'd find a nurse to stay with you, but under the circumstances..."

"Under what circumstances? How long have I been asleep?"

"Nearly four days. Let's just say I wanted to make sure my

patient stayed safe. Quite a few people in this household are angry with you. Besides, I have three patients right on this property, so it only made sense for me to stay."

Cody processed the man's words. Four days? Three patients? *Miguel, Luisa, me.* "Who is angry with me?"

The man chuckled. "I'd say the man you need to worry most about is Mr. Duke."

Duke? "I'm sorry. Can you give me more information?"

The man turned, joined his hands behind his back, and walked to the window. "It's not really my place to comment. Let's just say it's never a good idea to mix business with plea-sure, Ranger Steves."

Business with pleasure?

Juliana. Cody sucked in a breath, used his good arm to throw back the covers, and slid out of bed.

"Lt. Steves, I advise against this. You're not ready to get out of bed. If they see you up and about, they'll make you leave, and you need more rest."

"Make me leave? What are you talking about?"

A knock sounded at the door, followed by a scuff as it opened. Sheriff Gardner stepped inside. Cody's hand went to his hip, but there was no gun. Only long johns.

"It's good to see our patient improved."

Dr. Gold took two long strides to stand in front of Cody. "He's not."

"Looks like it to me. Get dressed, Ranger. We're going for a ride. Bring your things. You won't be returning."

"Sheriff, I won't allow it." Dr. Gold's voice was steel.

"You don't have a choice, doctor. I believe your other patients need you. I'll take it from here."

The doctor turned, looked at Cody like he'd just signed his death certificate. "I'm sorry, son."

"I'll be all right, Doc. Thank you for everything."

Doctor Gold nodded, picked up his black doctor's bag, and

placed a couple of vials of medicine on the bedside table. Then he left the room, his shoulders hunched like he carried a thousand lifetimes on his shoulders.

"Get ready. I'll wait in the hall." Gardner's eyes glinted. He might as well have said, *You're dead.* The door shut with a click.

Cody shuffled behind him and slowly, softly, turned the lock. He may not have much time, but a locked door was better than an unlocked one. Now, where were his clothes?

The tall wardrobe caught his eye. He opened the doors, pulled out his boots, his hat, his holster, his... Where was his gun?

They took his gun.

He shuffled to the window, which overlooked the garden. To one side, in the near distance, stood neat cabins where the hired hands—the ones with families—lived. Beyond that, the bunkhouse. The log buildings blended with the landscape so they nearly became a part of the forest, with groves of oak, elm and mesquite providing shade. The vastness of the property overwhelmed him. Anyone could slip in or out without detection.

There was Juliana, leaving one of the cabins. His heart skipped. She had no idea the fate that lay in store for her if she married Miguel. Dr. Gold passed her, and they spoke briefly. She watched the man walk away, paused, then looked up at Cody's window.

He lifted a hand in a small wave.

They stood there, frozen in time, sending and receiving a thousand messages. Or maybe it was his imagination. How could he warn her? How could he save her?

She broke eye contact. Looked at something out of Cody's view, and walked that way.

This one's on You, God. I'm in way over my head.

A pounding on the door drew him out of his thoughts. "Hurry up in there!"

"Sorry. I'm moving a little slow today."

Fortunately, no one turned the knob to discover the locked door. Which wouldn't take much to open, since Duke owned the key.

Maybe he could slip out the window.

No. Too many people out and about. His aching shoulder would slow him down. He looked around for something, anything he could hide on his person to use as a weapon.

The desk.

Slowly, silently, he slid open one of the drawers. Stationery wouldn't do him much good. Unless... He pulled out a couple pieces along with a pencil. Good thing he was right-handed. He adjusted the paper on the desk, using his weak left hand to hold it in place.

Dear Juliana,

I know you don't have reason to believe me, but I hope you'll consider my words. On the day of the shooting, I overheard Gardner talking to José and some of the others about taking over Duke Ranch. After you marry Miguel, they plan to kill your parents, and maybe you as well. At that point, the land will belong to Miguel. I'm not sure how it all fits together, but Gardner is working with the Fuentes family.

I also believe Miguel loves another. I'm sorry.

I can't prove any of it. I hope you'll take me at my word.

In a short time, you've become very special to me. Please stay safe.

Lt. Cody Steves

The Texas Rangers

He folded the letter, placed it in the outer pocket of his bag and closed the drawer. He still needed a weapon. The next drawer held a bottle of ink and a feather pen. He closed that one back.

There. In the third drawer was a letter opener. Not very sharp, but better than nothing. He placed that in his pack, along with the vials Dr. Gold had left, and closed the drawer. Thought better of it. Removed the metal utensil and slid it into the bottom of his boot.

He worked up a sweat getting his clothes on. By the time he was dressed—his shirt untucked and buttoned only part way—he wanted to fall back in the bed.

More pounding on the door got his adrenaline pumping. "What are you doing in there, Steves? Fixing your hoop skirt?" The knob jiggled. "Open this door, right now, boy."

Cody stood as straight as he could, composed his features, walked to the door, and opened it. On the other side stood Gardner, red-faced and flustered.

Cody smiled. "Sorry, Sheriff. Had to curl my hair."

A jab in the side made him immediately sorry for his comment. "Let's get moving. Duke's waiting for you downstairs."

"He's still alive? I figured you'd killed him by now. Oh, I forgot. You need a wedding first." Another jab stole Cody's breath. Why couldn't he keep his mouth shut?

He took the steps as slow and steady as he could, half afraid if he moved too slowly, Gardner would push him down. As promised, Duke stood in the entryway.

"Lt. Steves, I no longer have need of your services. I have to say, I'm not sorry to see you go."

"What did I do, sir?"

"What did you do? How dare you even ask me that question! I invite you into my home. Treat you like family. And you compromise my daughter and accuse my oldest friend of plotting my murder. That's what you did. If I never see your sorry face again, it will be too soon."

"Sir, I'm telling the truth. As soon as Juliana marries Miguel, they're going to kill you and your wife. You told me you bought out Gardner's father. I guess he's sore about that. But it's not enough for him to steal your cattle anymore and sell it for profit. He wants it all."

"You really have lost your mind, haven't you, boy? Look here. I don't want to cause you any trouble. I just want you gone. The sheriff's gonna escort you off my property. That will be the end of things. Against my better judgment, if you leave and don't come back, I won't report this to your superior officer. Ranger Smith, isn't it? But if I ever see or hear of you anywhere near my property—or anywhere near my daughter—you will never wear that badge again. You're lucky I don't kill you. Are we clear?"

Cody held the man's eyes. Any protest he made would only anger Duke more. "Perfectly clear, sir."

A movement to his left caught his attention. He dropped his gaze from Duke, then turned his head in the guise of readjusting his bandage. There, in the library just off the entry hall, was Juliana. In the shadows. He held her gaze for as long as he dared, begging her with his thoughts to leave. Escape this place. Because if she didn't, he'd be forced to return for her. Only then, it might be too late.

~

Juliana stayed in the shadows. Stepped out just enough so Cody could see her if he looked her way. Did he really believe that story he told her father? He sounded sincere. Whatever happened in that canyon, he must have heard something wrong.

Yet, so many things over the years had caused Juliana to feel uncomfortable around Sheriff Gardner. Little things. The way he couldn't hold eye contact in a conversation. The way he'd make a cruel comment to her father, then laugh like it was a joke. Gardner as a bad guy, she could almost buy.

But José? Miguel? The entire Fuentes family. They were like...well, they *were* family. Would officially be family, once she and Miguel married. What possible reason could they have for wanting to harm her? Harm her parents?

Cody adjusted his bandaged arm, then looked up at her. Held her eyes, as he'd done at the window a little while ago. What was he trying to say to her?

The front door opened, and Juliana stepped back into the shadows.

"Mr. Duke, if this young man dies, his blood will be on your hands. He is not ready to travel." Dr. Gold's tone was both stern and pleading.

Papa said something back, but his voice was low, and she couldn't hear. Soon Gardner, Dr. Gold, and Papa all talked at once.

Cody looked her way again. Reached in his pack and pulled out a folded piece of paper. Slid it ever so smoothly behind the large pot of ivy that sat on the entry table. Looked at her again.

She nodded. Held his gaze until he broke eye contact.

"Thank you for your concern, but I'm fine, Doc." Cody looked at Gardner. "You ready?"

The sheriff muttered a few expletives not suitable for a lady's ears. "I've been ready. Let's go."

The big front door creaked open, then closed. They were gone. She rushed to the front window and watched them until they turned the corner to the stables. Then she hurried to retrieve the paper.

As her eyes ate up his words, the knot in her stomach twisted tighter. Most of it, she'd already heard.

Miguel loving another? It wasn't possible. She and Miguel

had been each other's destiny since they were children. And he'd always seemed happy with the arrangement. Though something felt wrong about their engagement, those feelings were all on her side. Not Miguel's. Weren't they?

She folded the paper and slid it into her skirt pocket. Maybe Cody Steves *was* a bit off his rocker. Maybe this was all for the best. If that was so, why did she feel so unsettled? Her heart ached, refusing to believe the worst about Cody.

She needed to draw. Or ride. Something to take her mind off the events of this last week. Without a destination in mind, she started walking. Through the kitchen, out the back door, toward the open fields behind the house. Eventually, she circled back around the cabins, coming up from behind instead of the front, like she normally approached.

She cut between two of the homes. Miguel's room was on this side, and his window was open. Was that a woman's voice, coming from inside?

She stopped. Flattened herself against the wall, as close to the window as she could go without being seen.

"It won't be much longer, mi amor." Who did Miguel call his love?

"You say that. But once you're married to her, you won't be mine anymore." *Emily?*

"I'll always be yours. Nothing will ever change that. But do you really want to live the rest of your life serving those people? Oscar Duke worked for none of this. Juliana, either. If it weren't for my family, this ranch would be nothing. But if I marry her, it will all be mine. Then I'll make her go away and marry you. It will be ours."

"I know. I just don't think it's going to happen. She's never going away."

"Oh, she will. I'll divorce her, set her up with a nice little dress shop in Houston. With her parents dead, she won't want to stay here. Believe me. I know her as well as anyone."

"What if you're wrong?"

"I'm not wrong. But if I am, we'll just figure out another way to get rid of her."

Juliana caught her breath, held it, and eased back the way she came. She had to get to Cody! If what she heard was true, Gardner wouldn't let him go alive. If she didn't do something, he'd be dead before day's end.

Mama's words rang through her mind. *That's how I knew I truly loved your father—when I knew I was willing to die for him. When I knew I'd do anything for him.* Juliana could no longer deny her feelings. She loved Cody. She had to save him.

CHAPTER 17

"For among my people are wicked men; they lay wait, as he that setteth snares. They set a trap; they catch men."
Jeremiah 5:26

Cody could feel Atlas's tension as they rode. Or maybe Atlas felt Cody's tension. A muddy strain thickened the air and made it hard to breathe. Gardner led him toward the main gate until they were away from the house, when he veered away from the path, toward the coast. Cody didn't question the man. He knew as well as Gardner what was coming.

God, if I get away from this place alive, it will be because of You. I trust You. Show me what to do.

Around two hours into the trip, Gardner stopped and let out a long, low whistle. Soon, two mammoth men on mediocre mounts appeared. Cody had never seen these men. Wide-brimmed cowboy hats shadowed their faces, but the day was bright enough their features were plain. They didn't even bother to wear masks. This did not bode well. Each of them looked at Cody like a starved buzzard eyes a dying calf.

Cody nodded. "Howdy." What else was he supposed to say?

One of the men laughed, low and gravelly, and slung a wad of tobacco juice toward Cody. It landed on his arm. "Howdy." The man's smile revealed dark, stained teeth.

The other fellow looked down and away.

"Everything ready?" Gardner asked.

The tobacco slinger nodded. "Just follow Clem."

"Watch him. I need a break." Gardner slid from his mount and disappeared into the brush.

Fat sweat beaded on Cody's temples, tracked his cheek and neck. His shoulder throbbed. He needed water. A canteen was in his pack, but if he moved, they'd shoot him on the spot.

"You got any more chew?" Clem asked the tobacco guy.

He reached in his pocket and pulled out a wad, then held it out. Clem took it with grubby hands.

Cody inhaled, long and slow. "I have some water in my pack. May I get it?"

Clem answered to the other man. "Get it for him, Zeb."

Zeb spat into the dirt, slid to the ground, and dug through Cody's things. Pulled out his canteen and took a giant swig before handing it to Cody.

The opening was now covered in tobacco juice. Cody's stomach turned, but he took a sip anyway. Then another, longer gulp. It may be his last chance for hydration.

Gardner returned. "Let's get moving." He looked at Cody, gave a wicked half smile. "This is the best day I've had in a long time."

～

The Colt 45 revolver weighed heavily on Juliana's outer thigh. Funny, people called that gun the peacemaker. She felt anything but peaceful in this moment. She'd carried a gun before, but never with the intention of using it. Especially not on a human.

The sheriff said he was escorting Cody off the property, which meant they would have headed toward the main gate. At least, until they were out of Papa's sight.

But did they continue that way, or go somewhere else? She watched the ground in front of her for tracks. Why had she never learned to track? She'd grown up on a ranch, for goodness sake. All her life, she'd ridden these parts. But during those rides, her mind had focused on the scenery so she could draw it later. Or on whatever dress she was designing.

Papa always said she needed to get her head out of the clouds. He laughed when he said it, and Juliana laughed too. But now, she could see he was right.

God, show me where to go. Show me where to find Cody.

What had Cody said about the shoe prints on Gardner's horse? A V-shaped crack, with a little curve at the end. She reined Cielito in and climbed down. Looked at the path ahead of her. Surely they'd come this far, at least. She was barely out of view of the house.

There. A hoofprint. And another.

She walked back to Cielito and studied her hooves. Went back to the other prints. They were large by comparison. Must be Atlas's. To the right, she found another set. These were smaller than the first. She hunched down, trying to get a better look, following the set until she found one that—there!

She squinted. A V-shaped crack with a curl at the end. How did Cody notice that? As observant as she was with all things in nature, she never would have thought to look for such a thing.

Now that she saw the pattern though, she easily spotted

several more prints with the same mark. Cielito whickered in encouragement when she climbed back into the saddle, as if to say, *Good job.*

Everything in her wanted to speed ahead. But she had to go easy, or she'd miss something. With slow, gradual steps, she and Cielito moved forward, her eyes focused on those dusty tracks. Right now, they were her only hope.

Sure enough, a few hundred yards up, they shifted away from the path to the main entrance, into the brush. Would she lose their tracks? She followed their direction. Just inside the brush, a narrow passage opened up. Not much, but enough to follow.

She continued like a slug, inch by inch, looking for—there. Another print. She climbed down again, studied the narrow aisle of dirt. Only one horse could get through here at a time. Atlas's prints were more prominent. Cody would have been behind the sheriff. But here and there she found that cracked shoe print. This was the way.

After a time, the narrow path turned back toward the coast. Why would they go there? Blocks of ice encased her heart, crushed her veins as her imagination went wild.

No. She could not afford to lose her thoughts in what might happen. Right now, she needed razor-sharp focus on her task. Track. Follow the prints. Stay quiet. Don't be seen.

At this rate, she'd make it to the coast in days, not hours. Would she be too late?

~

Gardner clearly knew where he was going. Their fast pace jabbed Cody's shoulder with every step. His vision blurred, but he fought to stay aware. That was his only hope.

God, You're my only hope.

The thought that he might die today didn't bother Cody as much as it should. He didn't want to die, but he wasn't afraid to. Thoughts of heaven, and seeing his Savior, brought cool comfort. Seeing his parents, his grandparents...at this point, dying definitely had some perks.

But *Juliana.*

He had to live, to save her from a fate worse than death. From what he'd pieced together, they didn't plan to kill her. They planned to kill her parents, which would break her heart. And they planned to use and discard her. And if that didn't work, they'd kill her too, but not until she'd already suffered a crushed spirit for who knew how long?

After a long time—hours, though he didn't know how many—they stopped.

Gardner pointed his gun at Cody. "Get down."

Cody nearly fell from the saddle and pulled his pack down with him in the fall. Atlas blew out a snort. What would they do to Atlas? He was a good horse. Maybe they'd keep him. Care for him. Or sell him to someone who would. He could hope, anyway.

They led him through some brush to a small clearing. "Don't kill him. Just make him wish he were dead." Gardner spoke to Clem and Zeb, then walked away toward the coastline.

Cody still watched the sheriff's exit when a punch exploded his gut. Another hit landed on his jaw, and a thousand tiny rocks shattered in his mouth. Were those his teeth?

He tried to fight back, but he had no energy. No strength. After a time, he gave in and let them pound, pound, pound until the blackness closed around him.

⌒

*M*ale voices drifted through the saltwater air, and Juliana brought Cielito to a halt. Silently, deliberately, she guided the horse off the narrow path, far into a thick ivy-and-cedar-filled thicket. She slid off the saddle, her boots landing in a tangle of briar and blackberry bramble. Any other time, she'd have delighted over the fat, juicy berries.

"Stay quiet, girl." Juliana wrapped the reins around a branch, then added a rope, knotting it several times. The last thing she needed was for Cielito to bolt.

Easing the six-shooter from its holster, she held it gently, firmly. Kept her finger near, but not on the trigger. Tried to move forward, but her skirt caught on every thorn. Why hadn't she changed into dungarees?

She pulled her skirt loose, listening for those voices. One was definitely Gardner. Others she didn't recognize. She didn't hear Cody at all. After tucking her skirt into her knickers, she crept forward at a muscle-cramping pace.

After a time, she saw the back of a man's broad shoulders and shrank into the brush. Was that poison oak? With her luck, probably.

"How long we gonna leave him here?" The man slung tobacco spit into the ground.

"Until it's done." Gardner's voice drifted from the man's right, but she couldn't see him. "Wake him up." His ominous tone sent a shiver through her.

A shuffling sound. A thud. Then a groan. *Cody!* He was alive. *Thank You, God.*

"Open your eyes, boy." Gardner laughed, a wicked sound dripping with hate. "Oh, you can't. They're swollen shut. Well I guess you'll just have to listen, then. I want to make sure you're good and awake, to appreciate all that's gonna happen to you. Can you hear me?"

Silence. Then a low grunt. *Oh, Cody. What have they done to you?* She tightened the grip on her gun, ready to use it before they did something even worse to him.

"You thought we were gonna kill you, didn't ya?" The sheriff's laugh sounded insane, other-worldly. "That's not my style. I'm gonna let the buzzards do it. Or maybe the bobcats will beat 'em to it. You're bloody enough. They're probably hunched down in these woods, salivating at your smell right now."

Another groan.

Blood pounded in Juliana's ears. She couldn't cry out. Couldn't lose her wits. *God, help me. I can't do this without you.* She checked her revolver. All six chambers were loaded, yet something held her back.

There were at least two other men besides Gardner. One shot, and even if she hit her target, the other two would fire right back.

She couldn't see where they each stood. Chances were high she'd miss. She'd have three men after her, and what good would she be to Cody then?

"We're gonna leave you here for a week. No worries, though. I'm pretty sure you'll be dead by nightfall. A week's long enough for the buzzards to pick you clean. Then we'll come back and give you a proper burial, way out in the middle of the Gulf somewhere. Doesn't that sound nice?"

That man is insane.

"By the time anyone knows you're missing, you'll be fish food. And wedding plans will be well under way. Who knows, they may already be married, and I'll bring Oscar and Maria to keep you company."

It's true! God, don't let it happen. Show me what to do.

"Anything you want to say?"

Silence.

"I didn't think so. It's been nice knowing you, Ranger." Gardner laughed again.

She might lose her breakfast. Tears blurred her vision, but she pushed them aside.

Soon, she heard shuffling. "What should we do with his horse, boss?"

"Take him back to headquarters with you. We can probably get a nice sum for him."

Her legs ached from the awkward squatting position. Her heart hammered her chest. Scuffling. A horse blew. *Atlas*. Whinnied a protest.

Oh, Atlas. God, keep him safe. Foul expletives shot from three different voices. After a few minutes and a lot more struggling, she heard them enter the brush. Were they headed toward Cielito? Her heart froze in time.

No. They bore left of where Cielito was. If her horse would only stay quiet. *Please, God. Let her stay quiet.* Her heart hammered in her ears.

She stayed where she was for an eternity and a minute, long after she heard them ride away. Finally, she heard a distant blow. Cielito. Good girl.

She unfolded her body from her uncomfortable twist and crept forward. There, in a small clearing, was a man she did not recognize. Tied to a tree.

"Cody." The word came out in a whisper. His beautiful face...bloodied and battered beyond recognition.

His limp head turned toward her with a weak, almost inaudible moan.

"Oh, Cody." Tears clogged her words. "What have they done?"

~

*W*as he dead? The angel who'd come to escort his soul to heaven sounded like Juliana. Was that how it happened? Angels came? He'd heard there was a bright light, but he still couldn't see anything. He tried to open his eyes, but dried blood clotted his eyelashes together, and he couldn't pull them apart.

This couldn't be heaven. Felt more like hell, except for that voice. Those soft, ministering hands. That breath on his cheek.

"I'm here. I'm going to get you out of here. I don't know how yet, but..."

Cody tried to speak. His teeth...did he have any left? He worked hard to form the words. "My pack."

"What? I...I'm not sure what you said."

"My pack."

"Your...uhm... They took Atlas. I'm so sorry."

Did they take his pack too? It had fallen to the ground with him. He'd loosened it, pulled it with him on purpose, on the off chance they left him alive.

"Wait...here's your pack. What do you need?"

He groaned.

"Never mind. I'll look." Shuffling sounded. "Water. Of course." She held the canteen to his mouth. He let the cool liquid slide down his throat, his chin, his neck.

"Here's some medicine. Is this for your wound?" She didn't wait for his answer. He couldn't have given one, anyway. Her cool hands caressed his face, rubbed ointment on his wounds.

That wasn't what he needed. Where was the letter opener? He'd put that in his pack. Didn't she see it? She could use it to cut the ropes.

No, wait. "My boot." It came out sounding like *Mm mmmms.*

"I know it hurts. I promise, I will get you out of here."

Carefully, deliberately, painfully, he formed the words. "My boot." He got them out, but the energy it took felt like he'd just run a footrace.

"Your boots? Do you want them off? Here."

She tugged at the wrong boot. That was okay. When that

was off, she pulled on the other one. The opener must have fallen on the ground. "Ohhh..."

After a moment, he felt a tug on the ropes that bound him to the tree. "These are thick ropes, Cody. It's going to take me a while. I'm so sorry."

Why was she apologizing? If he got out of here alive, he would thank her with another of those long, delicious kisses. Every day, for the rest of her life. If she'd have him.

He drifted in and out of consciousness, thinking about that kiss. Feeling more life drain out of him every second, wondering if he'd die, right here in her arms.

There were worse ways to die.

CHAPTER 18

"Because he has set his love upon me, therefore I will deliver him."
Psalm 91:14

It didn't take long for Juliana to figure out that letter opener was no match for the rope. There had to be another way. She followed the rope, which wrapped several times around the tree, until she found a tight knot tucked into the layers. After some effort she tugged the knot so she could reach it better.

Cody hung limp against the thick rope. She placed her hand, ever so gently, on his neck. He still had a pulse.

Pushing the pointed end of the letter opener into the knot, she began to work it loose. At first, the tie wouldn't budge. After several minutes, she pried the knot enough to get the opener through to the other side. Her fingers were raw, but on she worked. The skin on her arms stung from poison oak. She could use a bit of Cody's ointment, but the vial was small, and he needed it more than she did.

Perspiration soaked her hair and clothes. Her skin was slick with moisture, making it even more difficult to work the knot loose. *Patience.* Gardner said he wouldn't return for a week. Surely she'd have it loose before then.

Cody moaned. A beautiful sound in the moment because it meant he was alive and somewhat conscious. She grabbed the near-empty canteen and held it to his lips. She'd need to find a fresh water source soon. But she wanted to free him first so he could get into a more comfortable position.

Her fingers ached from tension. She opened and closed her hands, grateful for the short break.

How would she move him once he was freed? The man was more than six feet of solid muscle. She couldn't carry him like a newborn babe. Maybe she should retrieve Cielito. She could use her saddle blanket as a travois. Plus, she had water in her pack.

"Cody." She whispered into his ear. She hated to wake him when she could only imagine the amount of pain he felt. But she didn't want him to wake up and think she'd abandoned him.

He groaned.

"I'll be back soon. I'm going to get Cielito."

Another groan. That would have to do.

God, don't let me get lost in these brambles. She let out a low whistle and listened. Cielito snorted a response. Juliana followed the sound back to her horse. This time, she scooped up several handfuls of blackberries and tied them into her skirt. The fabric was ruined, anyway.

When she made her way back into the clearing, Cody was still asleep. Had he wakened? For several minutes, she studied the swollen, bruised figure. His nose jutting to one side. Was every bone in his face broken? Would he ever look the same?

Tears blurred her vision. She knew better than to wipe them away; poison oak could easily spread from her hands to her face and eyes on contact. Instead, she let the tears fall, sucked in a deep breath, and grabbed the saddle, pack, and blanket from Cielito.

She spread the blanket just below Cody. He'd fall to the

ground when the rope no longer held him up. Maybe she could use the rope to lower him to the blanket, to keep from having to move him later.

An hour later, her fingers bled from friction, but the knot worked loose. She held the ends, gradually loosening the rope from Cody's limp body and guiding him as gently as possible onto the blanket.

He mumbled. Was that a cry of pain?

"I'm here. Can I get you something?"

He inhaled, then winced. Were his ribs broken?

God, show me what to do. She held the canteen to his lips. "Open up." Only a few drops...she didn't want him to choke. "I have some blackberries. Can you open your mouth again?"

He obeyed, and she dropped one of the sweet berries between his lips, and a few into her own. At least she knew where to find more.

Ripping a piece of her skirt, she folded it into a square. She didn't want to waste the fresh water in her canteen, but she could clean his wounds a little with some ocean water. The brush leading to the water's edge was thick and tangly. After some high stepping, she stood on the beach a moment and studied the view in every direction. Something told her to memorize this spot.

Funny how peaceful this place felt, with the breeze tickling her hair, kissing her shoulders. Like nothing bad could ever happen here. *I am with you always.*

She breathed in the salt air. *I know, God. But right now, I feel lost. Hurt. How could Miguel...? How could I know him so well, and know him so little? How could I not know he resented us?*

At last, she dipped the square of cloth into the ocean and made her way back to Cody. She gently laid the wet fabric on his eyes. If she could get some of that dried blood out of the way, maybe he could open them a little.

"Juliana," he whispered.

"I'm right here."

"I..." He sucked in a breath.

"You don't need to talk. I'm not going anywhere."

"I...need to tell you. Don't...marry..."

"I know. I know everything. Shhhh..."

"Juliana..."

"Yes?"

"Mmm..." Cody coughed.

"Hush. Whatever you need to say, it can wait. Get some rest, so you can build up your strength."

"Go...get your...father..."

"I'm not leaving you."

He shook his head, and the cloth fell away. He opened his eyes, squinted them against the beating sun. She held his hat, which she'd found flung on the ground near the tree, over him for shade. His eyes were swollen, but they were open. There they were—those beautiful golden eyes. The unrecognizable figure in front of her became familiar in an instant.

"Get...your father."

"When you're able to travel, we'll go to him together."

"No. Go now." His words were husky, weak.

"I'm not leaving you."

"I...I'll be fine. Tell your....father...none of you...are safe."

"But—"

"Go. Come back...for me. I'll be...fine." As if to prove his point, he rolled slightly to his side and used his right arm to push himself up. With a cringe and a flinch, he settled himself against the tree trunk. "I'll wait here." He laughed, a weak, pitiful sound.

"Cody, I—"

"Trust me. I'm too stubborn...to die yet." His voice did sound stronger.

She scooted next to him, against the trunk. Took his swollen hand in her own. "Don't hate me. But I might have given you poison oak."

He laughed again. "Hurts...to laugh."

"I know. I'm sorry."

"I'm not...allergic."

A small sense of relief washed over her. At least she hadn't made things worse. "I'll get my father. But not before I move you to a safer location. And I'm leaving you my gun."

"No need...to move me. You'll be back before...Gardner. You take the gun.

She rested her head against the tree trunk. She was supposed to be saving him. But here he was, directing her. "You sure are bossy for a man who can barely walk."

He grunted. "I told you not...to make me...laugh."

"I'll do as you say. My canteen is nearly full. It's just to your right. And in front of that is a pretty good pile of blackberries. Your ointment is there, as well. Now that I don't have to track anyone, I can probably be back by nightfall. But I *am* leaving my gun. It's a six-shooter, and it's full. Don't you dare shoot your-self in the foot."

He chuckled, and she felt bad for making him laugh again. She leaned over, kissed him softly on his purple, swollen cheek. "Be safe." As smoothly as possible, so as not to jostle him, she stood.

"Juliana..." His voice faltered, like he'd soon sleep.

"Yes?"

"Marry...me...instead."

Time stood still. She couldn't move, couldn't breathe. Was he serious?

Was this just a desperate plea of a dying man?

"Just...don't die, okay?" With a thousand prayers for his safety, she climbed on Cielito bareback. "Come on, girl." With a click, she led the horse into the bramble.

~

ody's battle to remain clearheaded was more exhausting than the one-sided fight with Gardner's thugs. In and out of consciousness he floated, drifting away while he struggled to stay alert. Had Juliana really been here? Had he dreamed that?

He was no longer tied to the tree. Beside him was a canteen, some berries, and some medicine. He only vaguely remembered her putting them there. He picked up the pistol and studied it. Pistols were fascinating instruments. He turned it over in his hand, then noticed the barrel faced toward him. He eased the weapon back onto the blanket, facing away from him.

His skin burned, and it wasn't from the sun. Could you die from a fever? He took a sip from the canteen and forced himself not to guzzle the whole thing at once. How long had Juliana been gone? Was she coming back? The trees swirled around him, and his head felt like it might float away.

The light faded. In front of him, the sun dropped, and the sky streaked hazy watercolor purples and blues and pinks. It was beautiful. If he felt better, he'd have enjoyed it. He wasn't aware of time passing, but suddenly it was dark, and the moon hung like a cradle in the sky.

~

uliana stayed in the shadows, in the tree line until she saw Papa talking to Dr. Gold behind the barn. What were they doing? It was dark already. When she emerged, they hushed their conversation. Had they even known she was gone? Knowing Papa, he probably thought she'd locked herself in her room.

"Papa. I need to speak with you privately."

Dr. Gold excused himself.

When they were alone, Papa looked at her as if seeing her for the first time. "Why are you out so late?"

She climbed from Cielito. "Can we go inside?" She didn't want to chance this conversation being overheard.

He nodded. "Stable your horse. I'll be in my study." He didn't even notice she rode bareback.

She led Cielito into her stall, shoveled some oats in her bucket and made sure she had fresh water. "Don't get too comfortable, girl. We'll head back out soon."

Sliding the study door shut behind her, she sat across from her father. He rubbed the back of his head with both hands, like his head ached. Did he look older?

"What happened to your dress?"

"Papa, it's true. Everything Cody tried to tell us. It's all true." She kept her voice low.

He studied her a moment, then leaned forward and rested his arms on his desk. "Why do you say that?"

As clearly and succinctly as possible, she told him everything. About meeting Cody that first day and feeling a connection with him. About the kiss, and how she was the initiator. About overhearing Miguel with Emily through the window. About following Gardner. When she got to the part about Cody being beat up and left to die, Papa hung his head, shaking it back and forth.

"He was still alive when you left him?"

"Yes. But he's in a bad way."

"Dr. Gold shared his suspicions. In the time he's cared for Miguel's leg, he's overheard some disturbing conversations."

"They want to kill you and Mama. Miguel wanted to marry me to—"

"I know. I had no idea. Juliana, if you didn't care for Miguel, you should have told us. Your mother and I never wanted you to—"

"Yes, you did, Papa. I'm not angry about it. But you did want me to marry him."

Papa's shoulders slouched like he carried a thousand years on his back, and he hung his head. "I don't deny it. I'm so sorry."

"We have to get him, Papa. Tonight. He'll die out there."

"We will. Give me a moment to put together a plan. Right now, I don't know who around here I can trust."

"I'm going to change clothes and get some supplies. Will you be ready by then?"

Papa nodded. "Get your mother to help you. Explain everything to her. Tell her to lock her bedroom door and stay there until we get back."

~

*C*ody slept some, a fitful sleep. A couple of times, he woke himself up murmuring and moaning, but he couldn't remember what about. His mouth felt bloody and strange. He ran his tongue over the empty space where his right top molars should have been.

In the distance, coyotes howled. The hairs on his neck pricked. As bloody as he was, they could surely smell him.

He took another sip of water. Felt around for the gun. Was he too fever-drunk to fire straight? Probably. He held the pistol in front of him anyway. He may go down, but he'd go down shooting.

Another series of long, slow howls shivered his spine. Were they getting closer?

The echoes faded into an eerie silence that lasted too long. Cody would take a noisy pack of coyotes over a silent pack, any day. He held his breath. They were on the hunt.

Can things get any worse, God?

Don't answer that. Just, please. Help me.

A high-pitched scream pierced his ears—Juliana?—and he

aimed the gun toward the sound. Tried to find the trigger. Before he could shoot, an explosion filled the air.

Had he shot? He didn't think so. He tried to focus on the pistol, but it was too dark to see. Horses approached. Was it Gardner and his thugs again?

"It's all right, son. We're here." Oscar Duke's voice was nearly as beautiful to Cody as Juliana's. "Just in time, too. There was a hungry pup just up the trail, and I'm pretty sure you were about to be the treat."

Cody wanted to cry. Instead, he laid his head back against the tree with a *thunk* that would probably leave a bump. *Yeah, it could get worse. But thanks, Lord, for saving me.*

Soft hands removed the gun from his hand. "Cody, it's Juliana. Can you hear me?"

His *yes* came out as a moan.

"He's burning up. We've got to get him to the doctor."

"This is my fault. Son, if you can hear me, I'm sorry. I don't know how I'll make this right, but I'm sure gonna try."

Cody didn't answer. He didn't care about making things right for himself. He just wanted Juliana and her parents safe.

"We'll get you back to the house, son, and get you taken care of."

He tried to say no, but his lips refused to form the word. Gardner wanted Cody dead. If he learned Cody was at the ranch, no telling what he'd do. And since Cody was in no shape to protect them, he needed to get as far away from the Duke family as possible.

Except, he couldn't move. Despite all his mental protests, strong arms lifted him onto a horse. Small, soft hands held him in place while Duke climbed on behind him.

One thing was certain. This nighttime horseback ride with a member of the Duke family wasn't gonna be nearly as pleasant as the last one.

~

*J*uliana's chest felt tight, like it might implode. How could any of this be real? *Thank you, God, he's alive.* But his fever was hotter than anything she'd ever felt on a human. Would he die before morning?

Blessedly, the fever caused Cody to sleep most of the long journey home. An hour before sunup, when they neared the house, Papa motioned for her to ride beside him.

"Dr. Gold is in the guest suite next to the one Cody stayed in. Ride on ahead and tell him we're coming. We'll take Cody up the back stairs. No one can know he's here."

She nodded and spurred Cielito ahead. Soon she, Mama, Dr. Gold, and Papa struggled to move Cody to his quarters. Before long, the house and ranch would be alive with activity. They tucked the patient into his bed moments before the sun yawned its pink-tinted greeting over the horizon.

Dr. Gold, working in the dark, placed a cool cloth over Cody's forehead. "I'd rather not light a lamp. No need to alert anyone here of an occupant in this room. I sent Cade with a sealed message to my assistant, asking him to wire the Rangers in Houston. They should be here in a few days."

The lines in Papa's brow deepened. "Can Cade be trusted?"

"I think so. But I told him I needed more medicine for Miguel's leg, which is true. I included that in the message, so there shouldn't be any suspicion."

Juliana pulled a chair near Cody's bed and held his hand. Could Dr. Gold fix his broken bones? She felt confident Papa would see to any necessary medical expenses. If any of them made it out of this mess alive.

Papa, Mama, and Dr. Gold whispered over her head. She silently absorbed every word.

"Doc, I'm sorry for doubting you. When you first shared what you'd overheard with me, I should have listened."

"I understand. It's hard to believe people you care about could turn against you like that. You didn't want to believe it."

"I don't know how I missed it...how I didn't see it."

Mama stood near Papa. "You missed it because you are a good man. Your mind isn't sinister, so you don't suspect others of such things."

Dr. Gold moved near Cody again. "This young man has a long road ahead. But he's a fighter. I think he'll be okay. I'll need some supplies to try and set these broken bones before they fuse back in place."

"Make a list. I'll see what we have." Mama sounded older than she was.

"We need to act as if nothing is out of the ordinary." Papa walked to the window, then back to the bed. "Since I don't know who I can trust, I'd like to avoid a confrontation until the Rangers arrive."

Mama pulled Papa by the arm, then placed her other hand on Juliana's shoulder. "Come on, you two. You need to get some rest. Doctor, I'll bring your meals up, and I'll check in every hour or so. Keep the door locked."

Against her will, Juliana allowed Mama to lead her away to her room. Once there, she removed her boots and climbed into bed, clothes and all. She tried to sleep, but her mind wouldn't let her. How could she sleep when she'd just learned her entire life was a lie?

CHAPTER 19

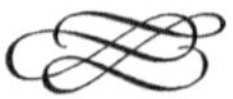

All Juliana wanted to do was sit at Cody's bedside.

They'd been back three days. Dr. Gold had set his nose, wrapped his ribs, and cared for his other injuries the best he could. Most of Cody's face was covered with bandages. What was visible was black and blue and purple.

And he still wasn't awake. Part of that was from the pain medicine. Would he ever awaken? Would he ever be the same?

With a slow release of a breath and a prayer for his healing, Juliana stood from her chair in Cody's room. For now, she had to pretend everything was okay. Had to pretend Cody wasn't there. Had to pretend she still planned to marry Miguel. Which meant she needed to spend more time with Miguel, checking on him, comforting him, swooning over him.

The thought made her nauseous.

She grabbed her sewing basket and took the back stairs to the kitchen. If she took something to keep her hands busy, she could avoid holding Miguel's hand. Sheriff Gardner and José stood near the stables, deep in conversation. They waved as she passed. She wanted to spit, but she only smiled and nodded.

Miguel's face lit up when he saw her. "Hola, mi amor." What a fake. How could anyone be so duplicitous?

Well, she would play along. Her life and her parents' lives depended on her. "Hello, darling. How is your leg today?" Her stomach roiled, but she revealed only a radiant, rhinestone smile.

"Better. So much better, in fact, that I feel like taking a walk."

"A walk? But—"

He pointed to the corner. "Crutches. I've already tried them out."

"Wonderful. Let me get them for you." Juliana set down her basket and her heart with a thud. A walk. The rest of the men were out tending to their duties, and the women to theirs. Dr. Gold would be in Cody's room, and he was slightly less cautious about movement in the daytime, when movement and noises would be considered normal. At night, he avoided lighting up the guest room to evade suspicion.

She followed Miguel down the steps, and he turned toward the back of the house.

"No!"

He looked at her, his eyes wide.

"Let's go this way, toward the pavilion. I'm afraid you'll tire easily, and you can rest there."

He chuckled. "I've rested enough for several lifetimes. Let's take a stroll through the gardens. There's more privacy back there."

The last thing she wanted was privacy. But how could she say no? Soon, they walked the path just below Cody's window. At the end of the walkway was a bench...and it faced that window. When they reached it, Miguel lowered himself and motioned for her to join him.

She'd just have to hold his attention so he wouldn't look up.

Were the curtains opened? She couldn't remember. If she looked, she might draw attention that way...

Miguel took her hands in his. She swallowed the flash of bile that rose in her throat and held his gaze.

"Let's get married."

"We are. You already asked, remember?"

"I mean today."

"What?"

"I love you. I know you have a dozen beautiful dresses you haven't even worn yet. Mama said you've even made some things for my nieces. They can be the flower girls. As for decorations, it doesn't matter how pretty you make the surroundings. No one will be able to take their eyes off the most beautiful decoration in the room...my bride."

"Miguel, that's crazy. I can't marry you today."

"Why not? Dr. Gold is an officiant. He can perform the ceremony. By the way, where is he? I know he's staying here, but I've hardly seen him the last few days."

"He's... sleeping in the house, with us."

"Not in the quarters? That's where he was bunked. Why the change?"

"I...guess Mama and Papa wanted him to be comfortable."

"I see. Come on, Juliana. We've waited our whole lives. All my days, I've known I would marry you. You've finally consented to be my bride, and I'm ready. Everyone we'll invite lives right here. Your mama and my mama together can snap their fingers and make a party. Let's do it."

"Miguel, I...I don't know why you're in such a hurry."

His eyes flashed. "And I don't know why you're not. Don't you want to marry me?"

Acid words tore at her gut, burned her chest. She clenched her jaw tight. If she opened her mouth, she'd never slow the torrent. Without thinking, she looked away. Up, at Cody's window.

Miguel turned his head in the direction of her gaze in time to see one curtain shift.

"Isn't that the room your parents reserve for guests of honor?"

She didn't answer.

"It seems like they'd put Dr. Gold downstairs."

She said nothing.

After a long, sour moment, Miguel reached for his crutches. "You were right. I think I've overdone it."

"I...I'll marry you. Today, if that's what you want." What had she done? She had no intention... But maybe she could distract him long enough to make him forget he saw someone in Cody's room.

This time, when he looked at her, there was no smile. Instead, his eyes held a cold glint she'd never seen before. "All right. Get the doctor. We'll do it right now."

"Right now? You said we'd plan a party for tonight. You can't expect me to get married in this." She motioned to her pink-and-purple, cotton dress. It was new. It was pretty. It was *not* a wedding dress.

He looked at her with loveless eyes. Looked at the window, then back at her again. "Tonight."

How could her blood freeze and boil within the span of a few seconds? Without a word, she nodded and left him in the garden.

～

Cody fluttered his eyes open. Was he dreaming again?

Without moving his head, he let his eyes wander the room. If he was dreaming, this was a vivid one for sure. It looked like he was back in his bed at the Duke's house. A soft snore turned his head to the right. There was Dr. Gold, in a chair by his bed, head back, mouth open.

How did he get here? Remembering made his head hurt. Still, he pushed through the foggy spaces of his brain to find answers.

Gardner.

Zeb and...Clem. Thugs.

Pain. So much pain.

The memories grew hazy.

Juliana.

Coyotes?

Somehow, he ended up here.

Again.

He had no idea who to consider friend or foe.

The doctor shifted in his chair. "Hello, there. Good to see you awake." He placed a wrinkled hand on Cody's forehead. "Your fever's down. That's good."

"You'll have to...fill me in on how...I ended up right where I started." Cody's mouth was dry, his voice gravelly.

The doctor crossed the room and moved one curtain to the side, just enough to let in some light. In a low, rich voice that nearly lulled him back to sleep, the doctor told Cody everything he knew.

"How long since I've been back?"

"A few days."

"Won't be long before Gardner figures things out. He thinks I'm dead."

"Won't he be surprised?"

Cody chuckled. It hurt and felt good at the same time.

A soft knock sounded at the door. Dr. Gold walked over and leaned close before opening. "Who is it?"

A moment later, Juliana entered, her face pale, her features strained. "Miguel knows."

"Knows what?" Cody didn't want to talk about Miguel. Just seeing Juliana was like sunshine after a sullen summer storm.

Her neck whipped his direction, and her face lit up for just a moment. "You're awake." Instantly, her eyes shuttered. "Miguel and I were in the garden. He saw the curtain move. He suspects something's going on up here."

Dr. Gold dropped his head. "It's my fault. I open the curtain each time I check Cody's temperature."

"He wants me to marry him tonight."

"No!" Cody pushed the word out with all the force he could muster. "That won't happen."

"I don't know what to do. I told Papa on the way up. He's gone to tell Mama, and I came here. All the doors are locked except the kitchen. Ramona and Juanita are there.

The doctor cleared his throat. "If the hallway is clear, I need to retrieve my gun from my room. I'll be back momentarily." He slipped out the door, leaving it ajar.

Juliana approached Cody as if he were a hungry lion. Or a dying one. "How do you feel?"

"Right as rain. Don't I look it?"

She laughed, a strained sound, but still beautiful. It was her laugh that drew him that first day. "You look slightly better than you did a few days ago."

"You saved my life."

"I... Yes. I did. You would have done the same for me."

"It's my job to save people's lives."

"I did what I felt needed to be done."

The tick-tick of the mantle clock echoed in the space.

If only he could reach out, take her hand, tell her how he felt. But he couldn't move very well at the moment. "Thank you."

"You're welcome."

Dr. Gold slipped in the door and shut it, ever-so-quietly, behind him. "Gardner is downstairs talking to your father. He seems agitated."

Juliana held Cody's eyes for a moment. He was certain he could read her thoughts. She was terrified. Angry. Ready to fight. Could she read his? Did she know how much he loved her? How he'd fight to his dying breath to save her?

She gathered her full skirt. "I need to check on Mama."

Juliana kept her back to the wall, just out of view. She was on the second-story landing, and thanks to the marble floors and great acoustics, she could hear everything said in the entry.

"I know he's in there, Oscar. You should've left well enough alone." Sheriff Gardner's thin voice was higher pitched than normal. He sounded like a man on the brink of a breakdown.

"Now, John. Calm down. I don't know what you're talking about."

"Liar. Let me see for myself. I know he's up there!"

"I'm not letting you in this house until you calm down."

Juliana knelt, made herself as small as she could, and peeked around the corner. Papa stood at the door, which was opened just a few inches. His body blocked the other man from entering.

"Calm? You take my prisoner, and you want me to be calm?"

"Your prisoner. What are you talking about?"

There was a scuffle, and the door slammed. Papa was still inside, thank the Lord. Outside, Gardner yelled. "You'll be sorry —you'll be sorry for everything, Oscar Duke!"

"What exactly should I be sorry for?" Papa hollered through the door.

"You stole my land, my inheritance. That land you bought from my father was rightfully mine. He could have stayed here, but you made him an offer he couldn't refuse. So here I am, left with nothing."

"John, you're a lawman, not a rancher. Even when we were

kids, you said you couldn't wait to get out of the ranching business. Your father knew that."

"I could have sold that land myself and been set for life. But no. You had to get your greedy hands on it. Now I have nothing. Emily has nothing. She will have her rightful inheritance, and you'll be sorry!" He punctuated each word like a punch in the gut.

A shot fired. Glass shattered. Papa's shout echoed through the hall.

Juliana screamed. Was Papa hurt?

Mama's favorite vase lay in shards all over the floor.

There was Papa, in the study door. He looked okay.

Where was Mama? Her heart thrummed like a dinner bell, announcing her presence. Her skirt swished too loudly, like it *wanted* to give away her location. Women's voices, tight with anxiety, came from the kitchen. She gathered the excess fabric to her waist and headed for the back stairs as quietly as she could. Her Colt 45 felt cold against her leg. She'd worn it constantly the last few days because it comforted her. It also terrified her.

"Mama?" Juliana whispered into the empty kitchen.

"Mija! Get in here." Mama and Juanita hunched in the pantry.

"What's happening?"

"The sheriff has gone loco, that's what."

Juliana chanced a look at Juanita. Was Miguel's sister in on his plan? "Mama, it's not just the sheriff. The whole world has gone loco."

Juanita held her gaze, her eyes wide and round with fear. "I've heard things. Not a lot, but enough." She shifted her eyes to Mama. "I want you to know, Mrs. Duke, I am not my brother's keeper. Or my father's, for that matter. Carlos and I have not taken part in any of the plans. You have been good to us. Whatever happens, we will stand with you."

"Where are your girls right now?" Mama asked.

"At the house. I have to go." She flew out the back door and would have slammed it behind her had Mama not caught it in time. She closed the door and locked it.

At that moment, more shots exploded from the front of the house. How many men were out there? She pulled her pistol from its holster. Mama did the same, and they ran to the front entryway.

Juliana postured for a gunfight. Would this be how she would die?

"Upstairs." Papa used his rifle to point upward. "I want both of you locked in our closet."

"I'm staying with you. Juliana, go."

"No! I'm—"

More glass shattered. A bullet whizzed past, inches from her head.

"Now!" Papa's eyes were wild, and she dared not disobey. She scurried up the stairs while another bullet thudded the thick stone porch wall.

At the landing, she turned to see Cade, Pedro, and Carlos, each armed with rifles, enter from the back of the house. "Where do you want us, Mr. Duke?" Juanita's voice shook from the rear of the entourage, keys in hand, herding Luisa and Isabella in front of her.

Juliana motioned for their attention. "Juanita. Up here." Instead of heading for her parents' closet, she returned to Cody's room. She held the door open for the girls and their mother to follow her.

The girls clung to each other, confusion and tears marring their innocent faces. Juliana wanted to comfort them, but she had no idea what to say. They may all end up as orphans today. Or worse.

Dr. Gold held his firearm close to his body. "I'm going down there. Your father needs my help."

"No." Cody's voice, though weak, held authority. "Stay on the second floor. Find a window. You'll have the advantage of height."

"Good idea. Lock this door behind me." The doctor left.

Juliana stared at the closed door until a rustling sounded behind her. She turned to see Cody sitting up, covers back. He wore his denims—thankfully!—with his longjohn shirt. He reached for the plaid button-up on the back of the chair.

"What are you doing?"

"I'm getting up. I'm not any good lying here like an invalid."

"You *are* an invalid. Get back in bed."

"Get me a gun." He had his feet on the floor now. "Tell me everything you know. How many men are out there?"

"I don't know." Juliana stood near him, arms out, ready to catch him. Gunfire pinged and drummed in the background. Her brain was in a cloud, detached from her body.

Juanita wrapped her arms around her two daughters. "Get in the closet." Once the wardrobe door was closed, she helped Cody into his shirt. Her eyes met Juliana's. "I'm so sorry. I know Miguel loved you once. But Sheriff Gardner...he's a bitter man. Several months ago, he befriended Miguel, fed him with lies about your father, about you. He promised Miguel he'd be rich, that he could own this place."

Tears flooded Juliana's eyes, soaking her cheeks. *Miguel.* Her friend. "He would already own it one day, by marrying me. Why would he—"

"Gardner poisoned him. Told him he'd never be the real man of the family, that your father would always see him as a hired hand. Once he won Miguel over, they talked to my father, and before long, Gabe and Isaac were in. I think Fred may be part of it as well, but that's all I know. Mama and I didn't take them seriously. We thought they were just being men, blowing off steam, bragging about what they'd do to the boss."

Her voice broke, and she twisted her apron tightly in her

hands. "My mother will side with my father. I know she will. Anna and Carlita will stand with their husbands, and they each have guns. Ruth took her children to hide in the woods. Please believe me when I tell you Carlos and I had no part in this."

Using the wall for balance, Cody moved toward the window. "Juliana. Get me a gun."

She handed him her pistol and positioned a chair for him. So far, the gunfire was still contained to the front of the house. "There are more guns in my parents' room. I'll be back."

~

Cody was about to question Juanita more after Juliana left the room.

But before he could speak, Dr. Gold stepped into the room. "They're headed this way. Get ready."

Cody spun back to the window, and sure enough, within moments several men entered the garden. Two were the thugs who beat him up.

Another was Miguel.

The man glared up at the window. "Ranger, I know you're up there. Come out and fight like a man!"

Juliana reentered with a rifle, another pistol, and a bucket of ammo. She handed the pistol to Juanita.

"Stay down," Cody told them. "You all need to go to another room. They know I'm in here, and this is where they'll—"

The window glass shattered, sending a shower of shards across the room, toward Juanita. She squealed and threw her hands up as she spun away.

Once the glass settled, he leaned toward the window and sucked in a breath. "I'm on my way. Just stop shooting."

"What? No." Juliana grabbed his arm.

Cody met her gaze, doing his best to infuse his eyes with confidence. "I'm not going anywhere. Just buying time."

Fear churned in her gaze, but determination too. "It's no use. They'll kill my parents and force me to marry him, and the land will be his. I'll marry him right now if it will make this stop."

"No. He'll kill you too."

"He won't. He'll divorce me. I heard him."

Dr. Gold inched toward the window. "That's not what your father would want, Juliana. Besides, no one can force you to marry Miguel if you're married to someone else."

"What?" Cody and Juliana spoke at the same time.

Dr. Gold looked at Cody. "I can't even count the number of times you called her name while you burned with fever." He shifted his gaze to Juliana. "And you couldn't stay away from his sickbed. You two are in love if I've ever seen it. No one can force you to marry Miguel if you're already married to the Ranger. And I can marry you right now. "

Had the man gone mad? Cody looked at Juliana. Maybe so, but if she was willing, so was he. "Let's do it."

She returned his gaze, but instead of love he saw...uncertainty? Did she doubt his love? A surge of adrenaline loosened his tongue. "Doc's right. I'm in love with you." Her expression didn't change. "I didn't want to love you, but you gave me no choice. Something about you *calls* to me. I'm lost in you. I will love you until my dying day, and I'm praying really hard that's not today. Will you marry me?"

Miguel's voice shouted from below. "Ranger! Where are you? I'm tired of waiting!" A bullet thudded into the thick outer wall.

"He's on his way!" Dr. Gold shouted through the open window.

Both men looked to Juliana, waiting for her answer.

Her eyes—those beautiful eyes!—glimmered as she met Cody's gaze. "All right. Only if you love me. Because, heaven help me, I love you too."

Joy sluiced through him, and he couldn't have hidden his smile if a gang of outlaws tied a noose around his neck.

"Do you Cody, take Juliana, to be your lawfully wedded wife?" Dr. Gold hurried the words.

They were doing this. Really doing it. He pushed up to his feet and stepped near Juliana, then took her hand and looked into her eyes, radiant with love. "I do."

"Do you, Juliana, take Cody to be your lawfully wedded husband?"

"Yes. I do." Her gaze spoke the same message. But then a corner of her mouth tipped, and she looked him up and down. "But we might have to wait on the kissing part until you're not black and blue."

Not as long as he could still draw breath. He pulled her to him and kissed her, ever so gently. In spite of the pain it caused, it was the sweetest moment of his life.

Until a bullet hit the mirror and shattered it.

"I now pronounce you husband and wife." Dr. Gold stepped back to the window, then pointed his pistol out and shot twice.

More shots rang from every direction. Juanita huddled near the wardrobe, humming a low lullaby to the girls inside.

Cody tried to see who was shooting. *God, help us. I don't know how we'll get out of this alive. Help me protect my wife.*

His *wife.*

The word sent warmth through every inch of him. It also gave him a new strength. He moved back to the window and held his gun at the ready. There were four men now, all shooting at the rock fortress that mostly sheltered those inside.

His aim rested on Miguel. Could he shoot the man he'd once considered a friend?

Miguel lifted his gun once again toward the shattered window, and Cody cocked. Before he could pull the trigger, a shot fired from behind Miguel, and the man slumped on his horse. Two more shots followed. Two more men fell. The fourth dropped his gun and surrendered to...was that...?

It was!

In the garden, Rett Smith slid off his horse and handcuffed the remaining man. Behind him, Evan Covington checked on the wounded men.

"Isn't it just like you two to ride in at the last minute and steal my thunder?" Cody called out the window. But he couldn't stop the grin that split his face, or the tears that soaked the bandages on his nose.

CHAPTER 20

The LORD your God in your midst, The Mighty One, will save; He will rejoice over you with gladness, He will quiet you with His love, He will rejoice over you with singing."
Zephaniah 3:17

Downstairs, Mama knelt over Papa, begging him not to die. Juliana knelt near his head, out of the way as Dr. Gold searched to find the extent of his injuries.

"There's an exit wound. That explains all the blood, but it's actually a good thing. Get some bandages. We need to stop this bleeding."

"He's still breathing?" Mama asked the question screaming in Juliana's heart.

"Yes. It's shallow, but breathing all the same. I don't know if there's internal bleeding."

Mama's wails echoed through the chamber.

"Be quiet, Maria. I'm fine." Papa's weak voice was music.

Mama sucked in a breath, then sobbed some more. "Don't you tell me to be quiet, you crazy old man." She let out a string of Spanish words even Juliana couldn't understand. Theirs was a love for the ages. Like her's and Cody's.

"Papa." She squeezed her father's hand. "Mama. I have something to tell you."

"Can it wait, mija? It's not a good ti—"

"She's married," Dr. Gold said as he stitched up the wound. "To the Ranger. You'll probably want to plan a better ceremony for when everybody's back on their feet."

Mama stared at her and shook her head as if she couldn't comprehend. Papa flinched, and Mama turned her attention back to him.

Of course, Mama couldn't comprehend. Even Juliana couldn't comprehend. Her husband was upstairs, talking to one of the Rangers who showed up today.

Her *husband*.

She left her parents and wandered outside. Her home, her beautiful home, looked like a battlefield. Another Ranger had Sheriff Gardner in handcuffs. The sheriff's knee was bandaged. He looked madder than a hornet on the bad side of a broom. He met Juliana's gaze, and hate oozed from his eyes.

She looked away. The terrace was littered with shattered flowerpots and broken glass. Around the corner, a woman cried. She took a few steps that way. Ramona and José knelt over Miguel's body.

The sight pressed into her with a powerful force. She may not have loved Miguel romantically, but he'd been a good friend. All these men who'd turned on them, she'd counted as friends. Almost family.

She dropped into a chair and wept. *Why, God?* She pulled her knees to her chest and asked the question again and again. Her mind couldn't form any words but those.

After a long time, the tears slowed. Her heart quieted. *I know You don't owe me an answer, God. But why would You cause this?*

The still, small voice she'd come to recognize answered her. *I didn't cause it.*

A scripture she'd learned as a child floated through her mind. *Be sober, be vigilant, because your adversary the devil walketh about as a roaring lion, seeking whom he may devour.*

God didn't cause this. Satan did. He planted seeds of greed, of discontent in people's hearts, and they grew like cancer. Miguel caught it. Now he was dead.

She hugged her knees to her chest and buried her face in her skirt. Today was her wedding day. It was supposed to be the happiest day of her life. How could she start a marriage like this? What kind of future would she and Cody have, with this as its root?

Had she been too hasty?

Had she made a mistake?

God, bless my marriage.

"Mrs. Steves?"

It took her a moment to realize someone was addressing her. She lifted her head to see one of the Rangers.

"I'm Rett Smith. Your husband is asking for you."

She stared at him a moment. Nodded. Unfolded herself from the chair and made her way back into the house.

~

A soft tap, barely audible, pulled Cody from his drowsy haze. He opened his eyes to see Juliana hovering in the doorway. "You don't have to knock. We're married."

"I suppose that's true." She crossed the room and sat on the end of his bed. "Papa was shot. Miguel is dead."

His heart ached for the pain that lingered in her red-rimmed eyes. "I heard. I'm sorry."

She wiped at her eyes. "I don't know what we would have done if your Ranger friends hadn't showed up."

"They were in Corpus Christi when headquarters received Doc's telegraph. Elizabeth Smith—Rett's wife—forwarded the wire the same day."

Neither said anything for a thick minute. For the life of him, Cody couldn't think what to say. A week ago, he had no end of things to talk about with this woman. Now they were married, and he couldn't wrap his tongue around another sentence. "I—"

"I was—"

They both spoke at the same time. "Ladies first." Cody nodded for her to continue.

"I was wondering...I mean...I know I was distraught. Crying about being forced to marry Miguel. You didn't have to marry me out of pity."

Pain walloped his chest. "Is that what you think?"

She didn't answer. Her head hung low, and her hair cascaded over her face.

Was he losing her? Cody swallowed a lump of anxiety. "Did you marry me because you were afraid?"

Again, no answer. *Oh, God. What have we done? Show me what to say to her.* Did she want an annulment? Could he stand it if he lost her? "Juliana, I won't hold you to a hasty promise made in fear. If you don't want to be married to me..."

"I...it's not that. I just...so much has happened. I don't know what to think."

Tell me what to say, God. I have no words. The silence between them stretched into a painful eternity. Finally, he gathered his thoughts, his courage, and the Bible by his bed. "I have an idea."

She lifted her gaze to see him, her eyes cautious.

"It looks like I'm going to be here for a few weeks. I'm in no shape to travel. Let me court you."

"Court me?"

"It will be unconventional. I can't take you on picnics or horseback rides for the time being. But as much as I can, I'd like the opportunity to win your heart. To prove I'm worthy of your love. Will you let me do that?"

Her expression remained blank.

"If, by the time I'm well enough to leave, you don't want to be my wife, we'll get an annulment."

She released a long breath. Her eyes showed instant relief. "All right."

Thank you, God. Now You've gotta help me win her heart from this blasted sickroom.

~

Juliana smiled at the scene before her. Cody may not be mobile, but he had certainly mobilized other members of this household to action. He sat in a chair by the now-repaired window, his guitar across his knees. At his feet was a checkered tablecloth and a wicker basket.

In the last week, they'd played board games, composed music, and he'd spent hours encouraging her dream of owning a dress shop. He'd ask the right questions at the right times, and she knew he was really listening. Really interested in *her* ideas.

Yesterday, he managed to make it down the stairs with Papa's help, and they ate a candlelight dinner on the porch.

Now, his grin made her blush to her toes. "It's a beautiful day. If you'll help me open this window, I thought we'd have a picnic. Al fresco." Nothing in what he said was inappropriate or suggestive. Why did he have such an effect on her?

She tossed her hair and her best smile his way. "If you want my help, Mr. Steves, you'll have to pay for it. With a song."

He threw a smile right back at her. Even banged up and bruised, he took her breath away. His bandages were gone, and only a little swelling remained. His nose was the tiniest bit off center, but it made him look rugged.

He strummed a few chords. "I was hoping you'd say that."

She lifted the windowpane and sat on the blanket, her hand resting on his foot. "I'm waiting."

"I wrote this for you."

Her heart soared in anticipation. A love song? For her?

He thrummed a few more measures, his eyes locked with hers, his expression intense. He took a breath, and began:

> *"There once was a cowgirl who whistled,*
> *She rescued me from a sharp thistle,*
> *She rode like the sky, delivered calves, and baked pie,*
> *And the cowboys all wanted a kissel!"*

Hearty, cleansing laughter spilled from deep within. How long since she'd laughed so hard she lost her breath? It seemed like years, but in reality, it had been only weeks.

The weeks since she'd last laughed with Cody, when he first arrived.

His strumming slowed and softened. He kept playing that way until her laughter died and she once again met his eyes. This time he sang new words...a new melody...

> *I am lost in you...*
> *Like a field of flowers in the morning dew,*
> *Like a star at night immersed in the universe,*
> *Like a mountaintop dancing with the moon.*
> *I get lost in you...*
> *Like a waterfall cascading out of view,*
> *Like an autumn leaf soars to the forest floor,*
> *Like an eagle glides through clouds beyond the blue,*
> *I'm lost in you.*

Juliana rested her chin on his knee. Her heart was full. He let the last chord echo in the room and fade to silence, and the two of them sat there, gazing at one another, each locked in the other's presence.

Finally, he whispered, "Marry me."

Love for this man swelled in her chest, tightening her throat. "I already did." She raised to her knees, leaned in, and placed a tender kiss on his cheek. She pulled back, only to have him capture her around the waist and draw her to him.

There they shared the most intimate, holy kiss—innocent and pure, yet white-hot with passion. It ended like it started, soft and slow.

He pulled back just enough to speak, his voice a delicious rumble. "Then marry me again. This time, in a beautiful dress you design and make yourself."

A smile tugged her mouth. "I wore a dress I designed and made myself the first time."

"All right, Miss Smarty Pants." He tickled her, and she wiggled to get away, but he was too strong. And really, why would she ever want to escape from his embrace?

She snuggled closer, feathered a kiss onto each of his beautiful honey-brown eyes, then sat back on her heels to drink him in. "I will marry you a thousand times. Any day."

A throat cleared behind her, and she turned to find her parents standing in the doorway. And for some reason, she wasn't embarrassed even a little bit.

Mama wiped at her eyes. "I guess I need to start planning that wedding?"

"I guess so." Juliana couldn't pull back the smile that stretched all the way from her toes.

Papa looked at Cody, then at her. "I'm happy for both of you. All we've ever wanted is for you to be happy, daughter. I'm sorry if we—"

"I'm happy. Your wish has come true." Juliana squeezed her husband's hand.

"We're sorry to interrupt, but we've just learned where all the cattle have gone." Papa moved further into the room. "Gardner finally confessed. There's a hidden gate on the other side of the Mustang Caves. They've been herding strays there for some time, altering the brand and selling them."

"So sending us all to the coast was a trick." Cody's breath tickled Juliana's neck in a most pleasant way. She felt scandalous for thinking about that in light of Papa's news.

"It would seem so. The rock tower was used as a signal for when they had enough cattle to take to auction. If it pointed to the coast, as it was originally built, it meant wait. Reversing the top stone's direction meant it was time to move."

All four adults paused as that knowledge settled over them.

Cody leaned forward in his seat. "I guess Gardner shot at us that day on the coast to throw me off track. He wanted me to believe we'd stumbled onto something."

Papa nodded. "I have some good news, too. We found your horse."

"Atlas?" Cody sat a little taller.

"Your Ranger friends wired from Houston. They spotted him at an auction on their way back there. They'll bring him to you in a few weeks."

Juliana closed her eyes and leaned her head against Cody's knee. She could feel relief pouring out of him. "What will become of Emily?"

"She's gone to live with her grandparents." Mama's voice reflected Juliana's own sadness.

"At least we know the truth." Cody kissed the top of Juliana's head.

"Yes. But at much too high a price."

Miguel's face—the kind face—the one he had when they were children, floated through her mind. How could she contain such joy and sorrow in the same heart?

"Enough of that." Mama clapped her hands. "There is a time

to mourn. But this is a time to dance. Finish your picnic, mija, and then come to my room. We have a wedding to plan!" She exited, pulling Papa behind her.

~

Three weeks later, on a Friday night, Juliana walked the center aisle of her family's pavilion on Papa's arm. Cody stood front and center, looking so handsome in a tuxedo, no one would ever guess he'd been bedridden just a few weeks ago.

The minister waited to his right, and on the other side stood Rett Smith, Evan Covington, and Dr. Gold. Standing up with Juliana were Juanita, Luisa, and Isabella.

Juliana was only slightly aware of her cream taffeta dress shimmering in the candlelight. Thousands of tiny mother-of-pearl beads lined the hem, the sleeves, and the off-the-shoulder neckline. A fitted bodice hugged her waist and hips, where more beads joined it to a flared skirt and train. The effect was simple, elegant.

She'd decided to wear her hair up, with her curls piled high and just a few loose ones artfully arranged around her face and neck. Judging by the look in Cody's eyes, he approved.

Tonight was the night. Her true wedding night. Tonight she would fall asleep in her husband's arms...tonight and every night for the rest of her life.

The ceremony was a blur; she vaguely remembered repeating vows, exchanging rings. She remembered applause when the minister announced them as husband and wife. But she had a vivid memory of that kiss.

That kiss—when he wrapped his arms around her waist, pulled her close, and barely brushed her lips with his. That was his signature, she'd come to learn. First, a barely-there kiss, followed by a deeper one, and then a third filled with passion and promise that left her both weak and empowered.

He kissed her, just like that, in front of everyone. She had a feeling more than a few heads turned, more than a few faces blushed bright red. Had a feeling, but she didn't know for sure.

At the moment, she'd been too busy to look.

EPILOGUE

Two years later

Juliana moved a chair out of the way so her rounded belly could fit through the narrow aisle in the back of her store. "This is where we keep the fabric, and over there is where the seamstresses work. I employ four, but I'm about to hire a fifth."

"I'm so proud of you, mija! Your very own shop, in the middle of downtown Houston. What a success you are."

Juliana's new little brother pulled Mama's necklace to his mouth, and she replaced it with his teething ring. Then she turned back to Juliana. "I brought you a box of baby clothes he's outgrown. He's more than happy to share with his niece or nephew."

Oscar Jr. squealed like he agreed.

"Thank you. I still can't believe I have a little brother." Juliana plopped a kiss on his fuzzy head.

"You think *you're* surprised? Try becoming a new mama and an abuela in the same year."

"Juliana-girl, you have four customers out front right now."

176

Papa entered through the paisley curtain. "Your shop girl is treating them all like queens. Where did you learn to be such a fantastic businesswoman?"

"From my papa, of course." She spoke to her father, but her eyes were focused just behind him, locked on her husband.

Cody smiled. "I keep telling her I'm going to quit my job and let her support me."

"You could..." Juliana winked. "But you won't."

"You're not wrong." Cody winked back. Above him on the wall was her cross-stitched life verse: *Delight yourself in the Lord and He will give you the desires of your heart. Psalm 37:4.* Right here in this room were all the desires of her heart, fulfilled. And every day, He just kept on giving.

Dear Reader,

I hope you enjoyed this final book in The Texas Ranger Series. My grandfather was a real-life Texas Ranger in the 1960s and 70s, and I've always been fascinated with their history.

Cody's character was inspired by my handsome, country-boy, musician husband. We both enjoy music, and the song "Lost in You," that Cody sang to Juliana in the last chapter, is actually a song Rick and I wrote together while we were courting. It still makes me smile and blush when I think of those sweet, early days of our love. It's even stronger now.

Even sweeter still is the love story God's writing with you. Every day, He calls to you, whispering His love, inviting you into His presence. May you enjoy the sweetness of His love every day of your life.

With affection,

Renáe

Don't miss book 1 in Renae's latest series, *Legacy of Honor:*

Legacy of Honor (The Stratton Legacy, book 1)

He's been raised to carry on the legacy.

After her mother's untimely death, Emma Monroe's dreams to become a teacher are dashed. She takes a job as maid and cook at the local Stratton Ranch, where she endures humiliation and hardship in order to provide for her ailing father and younger brother. Only Riley Stratton, her childhood friend and heir to the Stratton fortune, sees her heart. When she's asked to care for Skye, the young half-Indian girl most family members refuse to claim, Emma finally finds the purpose she craves.

Riley Stratton has it all, or so it seems. Growing up as the youngest son of the rich and powerful John Stratton, Riley stands to inherit a legacy of greatness in the Stratton Ranch. On the surface, his family looks like they have it all, but manipulation, deceit, and an ever-present quest for power leave him desperate for change. Yet his father has made it clear: do things the Stratton way, or face alienation and disinheritance.

As Riley and Emma choose between honor, dreams, and expectations—not to mention the love they can no longer deny—their first steps prove how quickly the situation can spin into danger. When their best efforts threaten the lives and hopes of those closest to them, it becomes clear the decisions they make will change the course of their lives forever.

Chapter 1

1882

LAMPASAS, TEXAS

Nineteen-year-old Emma Monroe watched the rain, like tears, make tiny splashes on the toe of her boot. Fascinating, wet patterns formed on the leather and offered a welcome distraction from the day's events. At least the February rain hid the fact that she'd shed no tears...not a single one since Ma left them early yesterday morning. If she let one teardrop loose, she'd never stop the torrent that would follow.

The preacher droned words of comfort. Empty, bitter-tasting words, for there was no comfort to be had. Ma was dead.

Yes, she knew Ma was in a better place.

But she didn't want her mother in a better place. She wanted her here. Now.

After several hours or minutes, she really couldn't tell which, the small group of mourners dispersed in a rising flood of black lace veils and good intentions. Emma nodded and thanked each person with duty-bound politeness, but she just wanted them all to go away. To leave her and Pa and Lyndel alone with the mound of dirt under which Ma lay buried.

An expensive-looking pair of shoes stepped in front of her. All this mud would ruin that hand-tooled, imported leather. She knew the owner of those shoes even before looking up into

Riley Stratton's warm brown eyes. She'd heard he was back in town.

Instead of taking her hands, though, Riley wrapped his muscular arms around her and drew her into a tight embrace. He didn't say a word, just held her against him, and it felt so good. For just that moment, she didn't have to be the strong one. For just that moment, she could lean the weight of her emotions on someone else.

After a long time, Riley let her go, cupping her face in one hand before stepping away, invoking memories of a school-girl crush that best lay buried with the other dead things in this graveyard.

At last, her wish came true. She and her father and brother were left alone with their raincoats, a shared umbrella, and a muddy mound of grief. But the solitude was only temporary. Back at the house, there'd be church ladies and cigar-smoking men and makeshift tables laden with fried chicken and pie, as if that would somehow make up for the fact that their world had just stopped spinning.

Despite her best efforts, a single tear slipped down her cheek, across her chin and down her neck. She quickly shut the gate on the rest. Not here. Not now. Not with Pa and Lyndel on either side of her. They had enough grief of their own without adding hers.

"I suppose we should go. They'll be waiting." Pa's voice sounded hollow and weak...weaker than normal.

"Who's gonna iron my shirts?" Lyndel dug the toe of his boot into the mud.

Emma pulled him closer against her side. "I'll do it."

"Ma always got the creases just right."

"I know. I won't do it as well as she did, but I'll try."

They stood there, even though they should move toward the wagon. Sugar, their sorrel mare, whinnied, as if to remind them she was standing in the rain with no umbrella. Yet none of them could seem to find the will to put one foot in front of the other, to slosh away from the last remnant of the one person in each of their lives who brought sunshine and light and joy...the one person who made life make sense.

Finally, Pa cleared his throat and pressed his hand to her back, silently urging her forward.

And that was it. They walked away from Ma, or what remained of her, and left her with the skies weeping her passing.

Riley Stratton had known Emma Monroe since grade school, but he'd never hugged her. Why would he? It wouldn't have been appropriate. But today, he hoped that simple hug said what words could not. He, unlike many of their age group, knew how it felt to lose a mother.

"What's taking them so long?" Allison's voice grated Riley from his thoughts. She strained to see down the road from her seat in the enclosed carriage. "It's raining, for goodness' sake. We gave our condolences at the funeral. Do we really have to wait forever for them to come home? We brought a cake. Isn't that enough?"

You could be in the house with the other ladies, helping prepare the meal. But he didn't dare speak the words. His sister-in-law was unpleasant enough without being challenged.

The fact that her own housekeeper and cook had just died caused Allison an enormous amount of grief, but not because of any sadness over the family's loss. Mainly, she just wondered who would cook and clean for her now. The cake they'd brought was purchased from the Sweet Things Bakery in downtown Lampasas.

"They'll be along soon enough." Colt sat beside his wife and chewed on his pipe. "It's good for us to be seen here. It helps our reputation with the townspeople. And we need all the help we can get, after Donnigan and his stunts."

The tension in Riley's jaw—from holding his tongue—found its way through his neck, across his shoulders, and down into his clenched fists. He had no desire to discuss their wayward brother, either. He'd rather be on the Monroes' front porch with the other men, but since it was pouring rain and there were no more chairs, he was better off waiting in the carriage. He almost would have agreed with Allison and suggested they go on home, but he wanted to check on Emma one more time.

He leaned his head back and closed his eyes. Sally Monroe. His mother's best friend since childhood. The only person Mom had trusted to keep an immaculate house and a silent tongue. When Mom died, Mrs. Monroe stepped up as a surrogate mother, at least when Dad wasn't around. She, more than anyone, made the loss of his mother bearable, the grief passable.

Now she was gone. It was his turn to return the favor by sharing the burden of grief with her family.

A clop-clopping from the road warned them the Monroes were nearly there, and Riley opened the carriage door and stepped onto the rocky path that led to the porch. He didn't bother with Allison—that was Colt's job. Instead, he opened his umbrella in time to assist Emma, then her father and brother.

"Thank you," Emma mumbled before taking her father's arm and guiding him through the maze of men to their front door. Her rigid neck and stiff back reminded him of their school days, when she'd try so hard to act like she didn't care a whit that he'd just pulled her braids or let a mouse loose near her foot. Only today, her stubborn posture didn't bring him any joy.

He rushed ahead of them to get the door, but someone in the crowd beat him to it. Pretty much everybody in town was here today...everybody but Riley's own father, John Stratton. Dad begged off, saying somebody had to stay and take care of the ranch, but Riley knew better. They had plenty of ranch hands. Dad just didn't want to have to be polite to Charlie Monroe.

Riley pushed through, nodding and speaking courteously to neighbors and acquaintances, trying unsuccessfully to avoid all the meaningless small talk that went on at these events. He arrived in the Monroe's parlor just in time to hear Allison, with her tilted-up nose and her simpering voice.

"Oh, Emma, dear. I'm so very sorry for your loss. Is there anything we can do? Anything at all. You just say the word."

"Nothing at the moment. Thank you, Mrs. Stratton."

Allison leaned forward and lowered her voice. If Riley hadn't been close enough to hear, he'd have thought Allison was offering whispered words of prayer and comfort. Instead, she said, "You know, dear. There is just no replacing your mother. But we do have an opening, if you'd like to fill her position."

If ever Riley wanted to wallop a lady, it was now. Good gravy, couldn't Allison wait until the grave was cold? He cleared his throat and stepped forward. "There you are, Allison. I believe Colt needs your assistance in the carriage. Go on. I'll be along shortly."

Allison gave him that you'll-hear-about-this-later look, but didn't say more. Instead, she did as he suggested and exited the crowded room.

"I'm sorry about that," he whispered for Emma's ears only. Her eyes found his, and he saw something both shallow and deep at once, like a boarded-up well of grief.

"You've nothing to be sorry for, Mr. Stratton. Your sister-in-law was just trying to be charitable, I'm sure."

"You're as gracious as ever, Miss Monroe. Please...will you let me know if I can help you or your family in any way?"

She looked to the side, out the window, then down at her gloved hands. "Certainly. You're very kind. Please, have something to eat. I don't know what in the world we'll do with all this food."

Someone pulled her attention away, and he stood there looking after her, helpless to do anything that mattered, knowing all too well the tunnel of grief she must pass through before she found light again.

He felt a warm hand on his back, through his coat. "I appreciate your coming today, son. Sally always thought a lot of you." Charlie Monroe looked small and weak, despite his better-than-six-foot stature.

Riley tried to summon a smile. "She was the best cook this side of the Mississippi. Probably the other side, too."

"Yes, well…" The man's lower lip quivered, and Riley looked away to give him a moment to regain control.

His eyes fell on Lyndel. Poor kid, sitting alone by the window, no longer a boy, not yet a man. Riley wasn't much older when his own mother died. For Riley, this was the second mother he'd lost. But today wasn't his day to mourn, as much as be a comfort to those who mourned more. Mourned deeper. Once again, he said the words…words loaded with sincerity but void of any power to relieve any hurt. "If there's anything I can do, sir."

"Thank you, Riley." Mr. Monroe moved to the next person, and Riley debated whether or not to speak to Lyndel. Instead, he placed a hand on the boy's shoulder and held it there a moment before moving toward the front door. He'd done all he could. It was time to go home.

Emma pulled the buggy to the side of the road to talk some sense into herself. Pa's words played in her mind. "You don't have to do this. We'll find a way. You should be packing for Baylor Female College. It's what your ma wanted for you."

Yes, it was what Ma wanted…for years they'd talked and schemed and dreamed of the day Emma would become a teacher. They'd finally saved enough for tuition, and Emma was to leave for college this summer and begin classes in the fall.

But Ma *wouldn't* have wanted Pa and Lyndel to be left behind with no one to take care of them. Pa with his bronchitis that seemed worse by the day. Lyndel only twelve years old.

No. Plans changed. She wasn't going away to college and that was that. Where she *was* going, was to the Stratton Ranch. Ma had been gone two weeks now, and the bills weren't going to pay themselves. Allison Stratton had offered her a job, and she was taking it. The wealthy Stratton family could afford to pay twice what Mrs. Wesson could pay at the seamstress shop. She wasn't the cook Ma had been, and though she knew how to keep house, she didn't have a clue about keeping a mansion. But she could learn.

She *would* learn.

She clicked to Sugar, and the buggy moved forward. Soon, she arrived in the big circle drive and stopped in front of the wide porch. As long as Ma had worked here, Emma had never been inside, but the outside always took her breath away. Thick, beveled columns flanked an elegant staircase leading to the front door. On either side of the entrance was a parlor-like grouping of white-painted wicker furniture, and Emma could picture the family gathered, sipping lemonade, laughing and dreaming like families do.

Riley grew up here.

No use entertaining thoughts of Riley Stratton. Hadn't Ma said as much? Emma would never fit into his world of servants and power and more money than she could imagine. Everyone knew a Stratton would never be interested in a lowly farmer's daughter. Ma had made it clear she and Riley were from two different upbringings.

Besides, charming as he was, he was also a scalawag...probably had a girl or three waiting back in Waco, pining for the day he'd declare his love.

She was only halfway up the steps when the door opened and Allison stepped outside. Her strained features fought with her pasted-on smile. "Emma...hello. May I help you?"

"I... Good morning, Mrs. Stratton. I was wondering if you're still looking for someone to replace my mother. If so, I'm interested in the job."

The transformation was stunning. Like clouds breaking to reveal a shimmery full moon, Allison's eyes took on a glow, and the fakey-sweet smile turned almost genuine. "Really? You want the job? Come in. Can you start today? Let me take your coat."

She led Emma into an elaborate foyer. The marble floors needed mopping, and a layer of dust coated the mahogany stair-rails, but the neglect couldn't hide its grandeur.

A lump of anguish caught in Emma's gut. These were the floors Ma had polished. The neglect...well, that was clearly the reason for Allison's sudden burst of friendliness.

"Come in. Don't mind the mess. I've been doing everything myself since...you know. And with little Davis cutting a tooth...and well, cooking has never been my strong point. I'm so glad you're here!"

Allison chattered as she led Emma through a lavish dining room that still held remnants of last night's meal. And possibly bits of last week's meals, from the looks of the dried-on fragments left on the plates. A faint scent of burned toast lingered as they entered the kitchen, where more dirty dishes covered every flat surface.

"Of course you know, you'll be expected to use the back entrance here." The woman's voice and attitude returned to typical Allison Stratton tone. "The carriage house is out back. Over here is the pantry, and out that door you'll find the meat cellar. The icebox is down there, too.

"We'll pay you a dollar a day, seven days. Please report at six each morning, and we'll expect you to stay until you've cleaned up after dinner, which is served at six in the evening. Somewhere I have a copy of your mother's cleaning schedule, I'll see if I can get that for you. Oh, and I have Temperance Society meetings in town on Tuesdays and Thursdays, so I'll need you to watch Davis for me then, as well as some other times during the week."

Emma's thoughts buzzed like a bee in a trash bin. A dollar a day? Twelve-hour days? Seven days a week...and on top of it all, she was expected to provide childcare?

Her mother made twice that and had Sundays off. And she was home by six each evening. Allison prattled on, and Emma knew she should show polite deference. But she was tired. She hadn't slept. And as much as she needed the work, she wasn't about to let the likes of Allison Stratton treat her like a mindless lackey. Besides, from the looks of the place, Emma was in a pretty good position for negotiating.

"I'm sorry, Mrs. Stratton. I believe you meant to say two dollars a day? I'm just making sure I heard correctly."

The prism of emotions that played across Allison's face might have been entertaining under different circumstances. Shock, then anger, then icy indifference, all in a matter of seconds. "Two dollars a day seems a bit high for your level of experience, Miss Monroe."

"I see. I'm sorry I've wasted your time. Good day, Mrs. Stratton." Emma pulled forth her sweetest smile, nodded graciously, and turned to leave, but not before a flicker of desperation and fear consumed the other woman's features.

"Let's not be hasty. I know you need the work, and as you can see, I need a housekeeper."

Emma paused, schooled her features, and turned back around to face her would-be employer. "I realize I don't have the years of experience my mother had. But her schedule wasn't as demanding as the one you just put forth. *And,* she was only the housekeeper and cook. You're in need of a nanny, as well."

Allison opened and closed her mouth like a startled codfish.

Then she tugged at her jacket and patted her hair. "I see. Well, I suppose you have a point. I'll pay your rate. But I'll expect you to earn it."

Allison's attempt at keeping the upper hand was comical, and Emma found she was enjoying herself immensely. She couldn't wait to tell Ma about it.

But she couldn't tell Ma.

"I'll be here by six each morning," Emma agreed, and Allison's smug look of superiority returned. "I'll stay until dinner is served and I've cleaned the cookware, but your meal dishes will have to wait until morning. On Saturdays, I'll prepare a meal for Sunday lunch, but I'll not work on the Lord's Day. As for your son, I'll be happy to watch him while you're at your meetings, but at those times I may not be able to get all my other work done, so I assume you'll be flexible on my duties, on those days."

The glare Allison gave her could melt an Arctic iceberg. But Emma was no pushover, and though she was grateful for the opportunity to work, she could make $1.40 a day at the factory in town—not that she wanted to work in a sweatshop. But if she was going to put up with the likes of Allison Stratton, she would be appropriately compensated.

Davis chose that moment to let out a piercing wail, and Allison looked like she might melt, or explode, or some messy combination of the two. "Oh, all right. But can you please start now?"

Emma smiled in what she hoped was a gracious and humble manner. "Certainly. I'll just need to see to my horse."

With a curt nod, Allison bolted toward the sound of the child's misery. Emma made a note to thank little Davis with an extra cookie, first chance she got.

Lost in waves of immense satisfaction, she turned toward the front entrance, only to run head-on into a wide expanse of chambray fabric, buttoned tightly at the chest. A slight tilt of her head revealed the shirt was attached to Riley Stratton.

"Well done, Miss Monroe. Although I fear you'll be wasting your talents working here. With your bargaining skills, you'd be better off in a boardroom somewhere. Or a courtroom. You could be the town's first lady lawyer."

Emma's face spiked with the heat of humiliation, though she had no reason to be embarrassed. She'd only done what was necessary to make sure she and Pa and Lyndel were properly cared for. Still, the idea that Riley had overheard her being so bold with his sister-in-law made her want to run and hide.

Instead, she took a couple of steps backward. "I'm sorry, Mr. Stratton. I wasn't aware I had an audience. If you'll excuse me, I need to see to Sugar—my horse—so I can get started."

To her mortification, he followed her out the front door like they were old chums. Which they were, sort of. But this wasn't a school spelling contest or a game of stickball. She needed this job.

"I'll take care of your horse and buggy if you'll talk to me for a minute." Riley's voice hummed close behind her.

She lengthened her stride. "Thank you, Mr. Stratton. You're very kind, but I can take care of Sugar myself. I don't want to trouble you."

Riley moved in front of her, blocked her path. "Look, Emma. Can we just lay aside the formalities for a minute? It's me. Riley. The fellow you love to hate."

That brought a little smile to her face, against her will. But she kept her eyes downcast.

"Look at me."

He stood so close now, she could smell his scented shave lotion, and the musky smell made her uncomfortable in a most satisfying way. Tilting her head back, she did as he asked. Or was that a command?

"I just want to know how you are."

She looked down again and moved to the side. She didn't want to tell him how she was. Saying it out loud made it more real. "I'm doing as well as can be expected, I suppose. Breathing in. Breathing out. Then I breathe in again."

"I understand."

Yes, he did understand. She remembered all too well when Mrs. Stratton died. Riley had been just fourteen. Emma was eleven. He didn't smile much for a whole year after it happened. But eventually, he became the same prank-pulling, mischief-making Riley, leaving a string of broken hearts in his wake. More subdued, perhaps...but time had healed his spirit some.

The way Emma felt now, she wasn't sure that would ever happen for her. How could her spirit—shattered in a million pieces, crushed beyond repair—ever recover?

"I appreciate your concern, Mr. Stratton...Riley. And I know that you of all people can appreciate what I'm feeling. But I really do need this job, and if I don't get in there soon, I'll be here all night washing dishes."

He laughed, the deep belly laugh she remembered. The laugh that caused many a wide-eyed, lovestruck girl to make a fool of herself. Good thing Emma had always had the good sense to keep her feelings hidden.

"Yes, I suppose that's true," he said. "We've left quite a mess in there. Well, you held up your end of the bargain by talking to me, so now it's my turn. I'll put your horse and buggy in the carriage house and make sure Sugar is fed and watered. Then I'm off to town. Good day, Miss Monroe."

He bowed an overstated, sweeping dip that was more circus clown than gentleman, and moved toward the buggy.

"Thank you," she whispered, but he probably didn't hear.

She started to return the way she'd come, then thought better of it and walked around the house to the back entrance. She certainly hoped Riley Stratton would stay in town a long time. Because if the feelings churning in her gut were any indication, she'd have a hard time concentrating on any task as long as he was around. She may desperately need this job, but she needed Riley Stratton's flirtations like she needed an abscessed tooth.

∾

Riley watched Emma until she turned the corner, head up, shoulders back. His heart nearly split in two. Watching her like this brought back all the memories of his own grief, as fresh as if it were yesterday and not nearly eight years ago. He felt that vice on his gut, squeezing away his appetite. That familiar anvil pressed on his chest, making it hard to breathe.

But it was more than that. He wished he could make Emma understand...her mother had been there for him when no one else was. He *grieved* for Sally Monroe. Perhaps his grief wasn't as deep as Emma's, but it was real, just the same.

He'd be there for Emma and her family, just as Mrs. Monroe had been there for him. The fact that Emma's eyes were the color of new spring grass, her hair the shade of sun-kissed wheat, and her dimples could coax a smile out of a bawling calf would only make his job more pleasant.

He climbed onto the buggy and clicked to Sugar, and his eyes fell on a lacey embroidered handkerchief. He picked it up, and the words stitched there caused his chest to tighten. "My daughter, my friend."

She would surely want this. It must have fallen from her pocket, or that bag thing women carried...what was it called? A reticule. He folded it neatly and tucked it into his shirt pocket, then guided the horse into the carriage house.

Ten minutes later, he walked into the kitchen to find Emma elbow-deep in suds, with one corner of one countertop cleared. "You don't waste any time, do you?"

"I thought you were going to town." She pushed a stray strand of hair out of her face, smearing bubbles in the process.

He wanted to reach out and set her hair aright, but he

didn't dare. What was his reason for coming here? Oh, the handkerchief. He pulled the cloth from his pocket and held it out. "I found this in the buggy. I thought you might want it with you."

Her eyes grew large, and she reached into her pocket, only to find it empty. "Oh, my. Yes. Thank you." She dried her hands on a nearby rag before taking the cloth and replacing it in her pocket.

"Your mother was always special to me…"

"Riley Stratton, I thought you left an hour ago!" Allison emerged from the shadows, and Emma jumped enough to nearly tip over the wash bucket. How long had Allison been standing there?

"I was detained." Riley started to thrust his hands in his pocket, but instead forced them to his sides and stood a little taller. He would not give Allison the upper hand.

She looked at him, then at Emma, then back at him. "I see. Well, please don't bother the help. We're paying her a small fortune, and I for one want to make sure we get our money's worth."

Riley just stood there, looking at his sister-in-law. What in the name of good sense had Colt ever seen in this woman, beyond a pretty face and form?

Maybe that was the problem. Colt didn't look past the surface. Well, one good thing would come of it. Riley would certainly never make that mistake. Not that Emma didn't fit the bill in face and form. She possessed more elegance wearing an apron than Allison had in all her diamonds.

What did it matter? Emma was a friend. Nothing more. There was no way she could become a Stratton. Emma was pure. Strattons were tainted. Emma was diamond. Strattons were glass. It was the coat he wore, the mold he conformed to, like it or not.

Other than trying to make Emma smile, other than lifting

her sorrow a bit, he needed to remove her from his thoughts. A connection between them could never work.

"Go on. Shoo." Allison waved him away like he was a fly at a picnic. Emma went back to washing dishes as if no one else was in the room.

Riley held up his hands in surrender and headed for his office. The trip to town could wait. He had things to do right here, right now. Number one on his list...pay a stack of bills larger than Miss Monroe's one-year salary. Number two...attempt to forget about Miss Monroe.

Number one turned out to be a far easier task.

Get Legacy of Honor at your favorite retailer.

Did you enjoy this book? We hope so!
Would you take a quick minute to leave a review where you purchased the book?
It doesn't have to be long. Just a sentence or two telling what you liked about the story!

~

Receive a FREE ebook and get updates when new Wild Heart books release: https://wildheartbooks.org/newsletter

BOOKS IN THE

TEXAS RANGER SERIES

Lone Star Ranger (Texas Ranger Series, book 1)

Ranger to the Rescue (Texas Ranger Series, book 2)

Lassoed by the Lawman (Texas Ranger Series, book 3)

ABOUT THE AUTHOR

This is the place where **Renae Brumbaugh Green** is supposed to provide impressive things for you to read. But since the most impressive thing about her is the fact that she almost won a car in one of those little fast-food scratch-off games one time, years ago, but she didn't actually scratch off the car until she found the card in her desk drawer, long after the deadline had passed, there's not much to say.

But if you really want to know about her writing stuff—she's the author of many books, made the ECPA Bestseller list twice, and has contributed to many more books. She's written hundreds of articles for national publications and has won awards for her humor.

She's married to a real hunk, and she's a mom to some amazing kids. She writes music, sings, and likes to perform on stage. She's a sometimes schoolteacher, a part-time chicken farmer, and an all-the-time wannabe superhero. Her favorite color is blue, unless you're talking about nail polish, in which case her favorite color is Bubblegum Pink.

If you want to know more or you'd like to read more of her books, you can find her at www.RenaeBrumbaugh.com.

WANT MORE?

If you love historical romance, check out the other Wild Heart books!

Waltz in the Wilderness by Kathleen Denly

She's desperate to find her missing father. His conscience demands he risk all to help.

Eliza Brooks is haunted by her role in her mother's death, so she'll do anything to find her missing pa—even if it means sneaking aboard a southbound ship. When those meant to protect her abandon and betray her instead, a family friend's unexpected assistance is a blessing she can't refuse.

Daniel Clarke came to California to make his fortune, and a stable job as a San Francisco carpenter has earned him more than most have scraped from the local goldfields. But it's been four years since he left Massachusetts and his fiancé is impatient for his return. Bound for home at last, Daniel Clarke finds his heart and plans challenged by a tenacious young woman with haunted eyes. Though every word he utters seems to offend her, he is determined to see her safely returned to her father. Even if that means risking his fragile engagement.

When disaster befalls them in the remote wilderness of the Southern California mountains, true feelings are revealed, and both must face heart-rending decisions. But how to decide when every choice before them leads to someone getting hurt?

~

Rocky Mountain Redemption by Lisa J. Flickinger

A Rocky Mountain logging camp may be just the place to find herself.

To escape the devastation caused by the breaking of her wedding engagement, Isabelle Franklin joins her aunt in the Rocky Mountains to feed a camp of lumberjacks cutting on the slopes of Cougar Ridge. If only she could out run the lingering nightmares.

Charles Bailey, camp foreman and Stony Creek's itinerant pastor, develops a reputation to match his new nickname — Preach. However, an inner battle ensues when the details of his rough history threaten to overcome the beliefs of his young faith.

Amid the hazards of camp life, the unlikely friendship growing between the two surprises Isabelle. She's drawn to Preach's brute strength and gentle nature as he leads the ragtag crew toiling for Pollitt's Lumber. But when the ghosts from her past return to haunt her, the choices she will make change the course of her life forever—and that of the man she's come to love.

~

Marisol ~ Spanish Rose by Elva Cobb Martin

Escaping to the New World is her only option...Rescuing her will wrap the chains of the Inquisition around his neck.

Marisol Valentin flees Spain after murdering the nobleman who molested her. She ends up for sale on the indentured servants' block at Charles Town harbor—dirty, angry, and with child. Her hopes are shattered, but she must find a refuge for herself and the child she carries. Can this new land offer her the grace, love, and security she craves? Or must she escape again to her only living relative in Cartagena?

Captain Ethan Becket, once a Charles Town minister, now sails the seas as a privateer, grieving his deceased wife. But when he takes captive a ship full of indentured servants, he's intrigued by the woman whose manners seem much more refined than the average Spanish serving girl. Perfect to become governess for his young son. But when he sets out on a quest to find his captured sister, said to be in Cartagena, little does he expect his new Spanish governess to stow away on his ship with her six-month-old son. Yet her offer of help to free his sister is too tempting to pass up. And her beauty, both inside and out, is too attractive for his heart to protect itself against—until he learns she is a wanted murderess.

As their paths intertwine on a journey filled with danger, intrigue, and romance, only love and the grace of God can over-come the past and ignite a new beginning for Marisol and Ethan.